BARMY IN WONDERLAND

P.G. Wodehouse was born in Guildford, Surrey, in 1881 and educated at Dulwich College. After working for the Hong Kong and Shanghai Bank for two years, he left to earn his living as a journalist and storywriter.

During his lifetime he wrote over ninety books, and his work has won worldwide acclaim. He was hailed by *The Times* as 'a comic genius recognized in his lifetime as a classic and an old master of farce'. P.G. Wodehouse said: 'I believe there are two ways of writing novels. One is mine, making a sort of musical comedy without music and ignoring real life altogether; the other is going right deep down into life and not caring a damn'.

In 1975 he was created a Knight of the British Empire and he died on St. Valentine's Day in the same year at the age of ninety-three.

GW00566722

BY P.G. WODEHOUSE
ALSO AVAILABLE IN VINTAGE

P.G. Wodehouse

BARMY IN WONDERLAND

VINTAGE

Published by Vintage 1997

2 4 6 8 10 9 7 5 3 1

First published in Great Britain by
Herbert Jenkins Ltd, 1952

Vintage
Random House, 20 Vauxhall Bridge Road, London SW1V 2SA

Random House Australia (Pty) Limited
20 Alfred Street, Milsons Point, Sydney
New South Wales 2061, Australia

Random House New Zealand Limited
18 Poland Road, Glenfield,
Auckland 10, New Zealand

Random House South Africa (Pty) Limited
Endulini, 5A Jubilee Road, Parktown 2193, South Africa

Random House UK Limited Reg. No. 954009

A CIP catalogue record for this book
is available from the British Library

ISBN 0 09 981940 6

Papers used by Random House UK Ltd are natural, recyclable products made from wood grown in sustainable forests. The manufacturing processes conform to the environmental regulations of the country of origin

Printed and bound in Great Britain by
The Guernsey Press Co. Ltd., Guernsey, Channel Islands

BARMY IN WONDERLAND

J. G. ANDERSON took up the telephone.
"Give me the desk," he said.

They gave him the desk.

"Hello?" said the desk.

"Phipps? This is Mr. Anderson."

"Well, well, well," cried the desk, baying like a pleased blood-hound on the trail of aniseed. "Good old Anderson! Splendid old Anderson! The top of the morning to you, my bright and bounding J. G. But this isn't Phipps. Phipps has stepped out to put ice on his head. He is sick of a fever. This is Potter, old pal. P. with an O., O. with a T., T. with an E., E. with an R. Potter."

"Potter!" muttered Mr. Anderson gratingly, as if the name had hurt him in a sensitive spot. He replaced the receiver and sat back in his chair. His eyes had closed. He seemed to be praying.

Each year when Summer came with flower and bee, turning the thoughts of red-blooded American men to vermilion slacks and parti-coloured sports shorts and those of their wives to one-piece bathing suits, it was the practice of Mr. J. G. Anderson, owner of the Hotel Washington in Bessemer, Ohio, to migrate to the State of Maine and devote his trained talents to the conduct of a more recent purchase of his, the Lakeside Inn some five miles distant from the town of Skeewassett. To assist him in his task he had brought with him this season, among others of the home staff, his courteous and popular desk clerk, Cyril ('Barmy') Fotheringay-Phipps, the young man who was out looking for ice to put on an aching head.

A discerning bird, flying over the grounds of the Lakeside Inn and subjecting them to a bird's-eye scrutiny, would have drawn in its breath with a sharp whistle of approval at the sight of them, feeling that in investing his cash in this desirable property Mr. Anderson had acted with sturdy good sense. 'His lines are cast in pleasant places,' it would have said to itself. 'Yea, he has a goodly heritage.' The lake, spacious and picturesque, was unquestionably value for money, and in addition there were lawns, trees, flowers, tennis courts, clock-golf courses and a Summer theatre, the whole interspersed with cosy bungalows for the convenience of such guests as might prefer seclusion to the camaraderie of hotel life. One of these last, the bird would have noted with regret, appeared to have burned down recently, for where it should have stood there was now a mere charred scenario still giving out little puffs of smoke.

With the sun shining, the lake glittering, the trees rustling, the flowers blooming their heads off and every room in his establishment occupied at a high rental, it might have been expected that Mr. Anderson, though short of a bungalow, would have been gay and carefree, counting his blessings one by one. But as he sat in his office this morning in late August, his brow was dark and his aspect gloomy. Even on his good days he looked a little like something thrown off by Epstein in a particularly sombre mood, and this was not one of his good days. He had had a disturbed night and he could not shake off the depressing thought that he was sharing the same planet with Mervyn Potter and Cyril Fotheringay-Phipps. As far as it is possible for one upright Christian gentleman to dislike the intestines of two other upright Christian gentlemen, J. G. Anderson disliked those of Mervyn Potter and Cyril Fotheringay-Phipps. If you had tried to cheer him up by pointing out that there was only one Mervyn Potter and only one Cyril Fotheringay-Phipps, he would have replied that that was a great deal too many.

A knock on the door broke in on his reverie, one of those cheery, exuberant knocks which are practically bangs. It was followed, even before he could say 'Come in', by the entrance of a figure at the sight of which, had his conscience been less clear, Mr. Anderson might have started apprehensively. He blinked and took another look, but still saw what he thought he had seen. His visitor was wearing a policeman's uniform, complete with cap, belt and pistol.

The face beneath the cap was one of singular beauty, lean, keen and finely chiselled, with eyes, slightly bloodshot at the moment, which over a period of years had shaken more women to their foundations than any pair of eyes since those of the late Valentino. For this was Mervyn Potter, the world-famous star of the silver screen, beloved by all except J. G. Anderson.

Deserting Hollywood, it being his intention to appear shortly in a play on Broadway, he had been a guest at the Lakeside Inn for the past two weeks, though to Mr. Anderson it seemed longer. It was the latter's considered opinion that of all the crazy, irresponsible pests ever sent by an inscrutable Providence to bleach the hair of a respectable hotel proprietor, this finely-chiselled mummer was the worst.

A female Mervyn Potter fan, seeing her idol face to face like this, would probably have blown bubbles at the mouth and collapsed in a swoon. At the least, she would have gazed at him with ecstasy. From Mr. Anderson's gaze ecstasy was conspicuously absent. His manner was bleak, bordering on the austere. We have mentioned that his night had been disturbed. What had disturbed it had been the entry into his bedroom at about 3 a.m. of this Mervyn Potter and Cyril Fotheringay-Phipps, the desk clerk. They had come, they said, to present him with a slight testimonial of their esteem. Whereupon, after a few graceful words from Mr. Potter, who seemed to have constituted himself master of the ceremonies, Cyril Fotheringay-Phipps had pressed into Mr. Anderson's hand a large, slimy, wriggling frog.

They had then withdrawn, laughing heartily, like a couple of intoxicated ambassadors who have delivered their credentials to a reigning monarch and are off to get a few more quick ones before the bars close.

It is a very lenient employer of labour who can view with equanimity conduct of this description in a minor member of his staff. Cyril Fotheringay-Phipps was an excellent desk clerk, polite and painstaking and with a good desk-side manner, but a blameless record over the space of two years was not enough to save him from the lightning of Mr. Anderson's wrath after goings-on like last night's goings-on. Legal red tape prevented Mr. Anderson doing what he would have liked to do—viz. skin Cyril Fotheringay-Phipps with a rusty knife and dip him in boiling oil, but within his limitations he proposed to deal faithfully with him.

Their relationship of hotel proprietor and guest made it impossible for him to do the same in the case of Mervyn Potter, but he could give him a nasty look, and he did so. It was a look that seemed to bring into the office an Edgar Allan Poe-like atmosphere of wailing winds and family curses.

"Good morning," he said stiffly.

"Good morning, good morning, good morning, good morning,"

said Mervyn Potter, taking a chair and one of Mr. Anderson's cigarettes and placing in his buttonhole a rose from the vase on Mr. Anderson's desk. If there was a sunnier man than this refugee from Hollywood within a radius of fifty miles of the Lakeside Inn, it would have required a long search to find him. "What a beautiful world it is, is it not? One of the nicest I ever came across. But you are wondering why I am here, no doubt, though delighted, of course, to see me. Well, when we were chatting on the telephone just now—and what a wonderful invention that is, the telephone. Good brains there I always say when they bring up the subject of Alexander Graham Bell—I suddenly remembered that there was something I wanted to tell you. Not that it was a beautiful world. Something else. Some little secret that I wanted to share with you. So up I came, going hoppity-hoppity-hop."

A disturbing thought struck Mr. Anderson.

"You haven't been sitting at the desk, dressed like that?"

"I have indeed," said the human sunbeam, blowing a jovial smoke-ring, "and I was a sensational success. It was pretty to see my public's enthusiasm. I got writer's cramp, signing autographs. This costume is part and parcel of my story. Anderson, my poor old deadbeat, you have had a bereavement. I burned my bungalow down last night."

The stony expression on Mr. Anderson's face became intensified. He might have been something Gutzon Borglum had carved on the side of a mountain. As so often when in Mervyn Potter's society, he was trying to think who it was that he reminded himself of. Then he got it. Job. Job after he had lost his camels and acquired all those boils. Not that Job's sorrows could be compared with those of a man forced to associate with Mervyn Potter.

"So I am informed," he said curtly.

"Ah, they don't keep things from you? They come running to the boss with their little troubles, do they? Capital, capital. I like this spirit of confidence and frankness."

"You were smoking in bed, no doubt?"

"That would seem to be a fair inference from the known facts," assented Mervyn Potter, adjusting the rose in his buttonhole and taking another of Mr. Anderson's cigarettes. "I was also, if I am not gravely mistaken, somewhat pie-eyed. I got engaged to be married yesterday, and you know how it is when the heart is young and the laughing love god doing his stuff. You dance. You sing. You get the party spirit. You reach out for the blushful Hippocrene and celebrate till your eyes bubble. Ah, love, love!" said Mervyn Potter. "Is there anything like it, J. G. Anderson? But I mustn't take up your time with a lover's rhapsodies. You are all agog to hear about the sinister affair of the burning bungalow. Stripping the thing to its bare essentials and omitting all tedious preliminaries, I awoke from a refreshing sleep to find a hell of a conflagration in progress and myself being hauled out of it by that admirable young man, Cyril Phipps."

"That what?" said Mr. Anderson.

"He had apparently observed the doings from his bedroom window and thought it wise to step across and lend a hand. It was a close call. Now that I have had leisure to reconstruct the scene, I remember waking up and feeling a sort of genial glow and seeing flames leaping hither and thither about the bedchamber, but it didn't occur to me that there was anything I could do about it, and I had just curled up and dozed off again, when in rushed this visiting fireman and extracted me from the sheets like a cork out of a bottle. I was rather annoyed at the time, I recollect, because, unlike the heroine of 'I'm to be Queen of the May, Mother', a poem which is no doubt constantly on your lips, I object to being called early. But I can see now that it was most fortunate."

"Fortunate?" said Mr. Anderson.

"Another minute or two, and you would have lost me."

"Yes," said Mr. Anderson.

Mervyn Potter took another cigarette.

"Although I say it myself," he proceeded, "I think I showed up pretty well under these testing conditions. Many men in such a situation, finding themselves in the process of being toasted like a Welsh rarebit, would have lost their heads, but I kept my presence of mind and saved a couple of bottles of whisky. My wardrobe perished in the holocaust, of course. When you're being given the sleeve across the windpipe by Acts of God, you don't waste time fumbling around for socks and trousers. I stood not upon the order of my going, but got out in my pink pyjamas. That is why you see me now in what may appear to you fancy dress. I broke into your Summer theatre and borrowed this costume from one of the dressing-rooms. After which we repaired to Phipps's boudoir and started in on the wassail bowl. There are moments when one needs a drink. Are there moments, indeed, when one doesn't? Well, there you are, Toots," said Mervyn Potter, rising. "That's all I came to tell you."

An animal snarl escaped Mr. Anderson. He had remained silent while his visitor was speaking, because the other was a difficult man to interrupt. Seeing an opportunity now of getting a word in edgeways, he seized it.

"Indeed? I thought you might possibly have come to explain your behaviour of last night."

Mervyn Potter wrinkled his forehead. It was plain that he was at a loss.

"Last night? Behaviour?"

"You have forgotten the incident?" said Mr. Anderson, gnashing his teeth slightly. "To refresh your memory, at three o'clock this morning, accompanied by my desk clerk, you invaded my bedroom and gave me a frog."

Mervyn Potter's face cleared.

"Of course, yes. It all comes back to me. My dear fellow, we want no thanks. Keep that frog, J. G. Anderson, and make of it a constant companion. I thought Phipps was looking very well, didn't you?"

"I beg your pardon?"

"Last night. Very rosy, he seemed to me. The pure Maine air and your fatherly care have done wonders for him. When I met him in London two years ago, he seemed to me a little peaked. I was over there making a picture and the Drones Club gave me a dinner at which he was in the chair, and of course we fraternized. We got on together like a couple of Warner Brothers. Charming chap. His name's really Fotheringay-Phipps. Did you know? One of those hyphenated things. How did you and he happen to come together, by the way? It's a long long trail from London to Skeewassett, Maine."

Mr. Anderson was feeling far from in the mood to sit chatting with Mervyn Potter about Cyril Fotheringay-Phipps, one of the most nauseous topics it would have been possible to select, and this lent an additional coldness to his manner.

"As you appear interested and seem to have plenty of time on your hands for casual conversation, which I may mention is not the case with me, and . . . er . . ."

"Start again," advised Mervyn Potter.

Mr. Anderson counted ten slowly. His doctor, anxious about his blood pressure, had recommended this stratagem in times of

stress. The great thing on these occasions when some pest has
cornered you and is making you hot under the collar and all
steamed up, his doctor had said, is to be calm ... calm. Otherwise,
he had gone on to explain, you come unstuck at the seams, get
apoplexy, and before you can say 'What ho' spin round in a
circle and hand in your dinner pail. These medical men express
themselves oddly.

"Two years ago," he said, speaking carefully so that his
remarks would be clear and would not have to be repeated,
"I made the acquaintance of Phipps's uncle, Lord Binghampton.
Lord Binghampton," said Mr. Anderson, still spacing his words
carefully, "breeds Siamese cats. The annual convention of the
American Siamese Cat Breeders Association was taking place in
Bessemer that year. Lord Binghampton, being in New York,
visiting his father-in-law, decided to attend the convention. He
stayed at my hotel."

"All the other hotels full, eh?" said Mervyn Potter, seeing a
possible explanation of this eccentric behaviour.

Mr. Anderson counted ten once more, rather more slowly than
the first time.

"We became acquainted. He told me that he had a nephew
in England for whom he was trying to find occupation, and
persuaded me to engage him as a desk clerk," said Mr. Anderson,
his face darkening as he thought of the rash act into which he had
allowed himself to be cajoled by that silver-tongued Briton. It
had resulted, as so many rash acts result, from a good dinner
which had left him mellow and co-operative, and he was
wondering now how he could ever have become as mellow and
co-operative as that, even after a banquet of Lucullus.

Mervyn Potter nodded.

"I see. So that's how it came about. I was surprised to find
him here."

"You won't find him here much longer." Mr. Anderson took
up the telephone. "Give me the desk . . . Phipps? This is Mr.
Anderson. Come to my office immediately."

Mervyn Potter shook his head disapprovingly.

"What do you want Phipps for? He can add nothing to my
story. Besides, he needs complete repose this morning. He has a
headache."

"I'll make it worse," said Mr. Anderson, grimly replacing the
receiver.

For the first time, the sombreness of his companion's demeanour seemed to impress itself on the motion picture star.

"From a certain guarded something in your manner, I gather that Phipps has incurred your displeasure."

"He has."

"You feel he was a bit informal last night?"

"I do."

"You are thinking of firing him?"

"I am."

Mervyn Potter laughed amusedly.

"There is no terror, J. G. Anderson, in your threats, for Phipps is armed so strong in honesty that they pass by him like the idle wind, which he respects not. Fire him, forsooth! Why, he's probably on his way up here now to spit in your eye and hand in his resignation. He's come into money."

"What!"

"Some sort of deceased grandfather, if I got the story right. A millionaire, I believe. So you can readily understand why he was feeling a bit above himself last night. He had had the news in the afternoon. And as I had plighted my troth that same afternoon to a girl whom it would be conservative to call a pippin, you can understand why I was feeling a bit above myself. I hope I am not making this too abstruse for you? You have the picture clear? Phipps, on the one hand, in excellent fettle because of his sudden wealth, I, on the other, in excellent fettle because love had found the way. Both in excellent fettle."

If the bird to which we alluded earlier had happened to seize this moment to perch on Mr. Anderson's window-sill and look in, it would have observed a remarkable change for the better taking place in the hotel proprietor's aspect, starting on the cue 'come into money'. His resemblance to an Epstein statue had vanished, leaving him a softer, kindlier J. G. Anderson.

"Well, I'll be darned," he said, and his voice was virtually a coo, as if he had been a cushat dove in conference with another cushat dove. "Come into money, has he? Much?"

"Wealth beyond the dreams of avarice, I gathered. That's why he let you have that frog. 'See, Potter,' said Phipps, ducking under a bush and coming up with the batrachian, if batrachian is the word I want: 'A fine frog. Come in useful, this will.' 'You are going to keep it?' I said. 'Of course I am going to keep it,' he replied, adding that he proposed to teach it a few simple tricks and get it dates on television. Well, I talked him out of that. 'What do you need with performing frogs, Phipps?' I said. 'You are rich. Be broad, be generous. Share the wealth. Many a poor man would be glad of this frog. Give of your plenty, Phipps,' I said. And after a certain amount of argument he saw my point and, your name happening to come up, he consented to hand it over to you. He said you were a priceless old stinker who in a less tolerant community would years ago have been shot at sunrise, but that your need was greater than his. I thought it showed a nice spirit in the lad. And now I really must be tearing myself away. I have to go to Skeewassett to replenish my wardrobe. Did I mention," said Mervyn Potter, rising from the desk on which he had been sitting, "that this was a beautiful world? I did? Then I have nothing more to add. A very hearty good morning to you, J. G. Anderson."

⋆ 2 ⋆

For some moments after his visitor had left him, Mr. Anderson sat musing. And though he was musing on Cyril Fotheringay-Phipps, he experienced none of that shrinking horror which had distressed him when musing on Cyril Fotheringay-Phipps before, causing him to feel, as he examined Cyril Fotheringay-Phipps's soul, as if he were peering into some black abyss with hissing snakes at the bottom of it. The thought had floated into his mind like drifting thistledown that, given a little service and co-operation, here was his chance of severing his connection with the Hotel Washington and the town of Bessemer, Ohio.

Towns like Bessemer, Ohio, are all right, if you like towns like Bessemer, Ohio, but they have this defect, that in the winter months they tend to get a bit chilly, and Mr. Anderson, as the years went by and his blood grew thinner, had come more and more to feel how agreeable a move to a warmer climate would be. If he could get the Washington off his hands, he could buy some nice little hotel in Florida and retire there when the snows began to fly. The Lakeside Inn during the summer, and the nice little hotel in Florida for the winter . . . what pleasanter life could a man who suffered from chilblains have? And who more suitable to take the Washington off his hands than an ambitious young desk clerk who had just inherited a vast fortune? For the first time that morning Mr. Anderson found himself seeing eye to eye with Mervyn Potter and agreeing with him that this was a beautiful world. Mervyn Potter, in his opinion, had in no way exaggerated its charms.

He had fallen into a roseate daydream and was within an ace of humming a gay tune when, as had happened previously, his reverie was broken by a knock on the door, but this time a meek, deprecating knock like the apologetic scratching noise which a dog makes when returning to the old home after having been out all night hunting. Cyril Fotheringay-Phipps sidled in, giving at the knees a little as he always did when entering the presence of

16

the big chief. Wealth beyond the dreams of avarice might have come to Cyril Phipps, but J. G. Anderson still scared the daylights out of him.

Cyril Phipps was tall and willowy, a young Englishman of the type so common in the Drones Club, Dover Street, London, an institution of which, though it was now two years since he had enrolled himself under Mr. Anderson's banner, he remained a member in good standing. His disposition was intensely amiable, his hair the colour of creamery butter and his face one of those open, engaging faces which arouse the maternal instinct in women but, for these things cut both ways, incline male employers whose livers sometimes trouble them of a morning to be brusque and irascible. On days when he was not feeling quite himself, J. G. Anderson found the sight of that mild, deferential face infuriating and was apt to touch on the fact in his conversation.

On his good mornings he was able to console himself with the reflection that this desk clerk of his, though handicapped, in his opinion, by an I.Q. somewhat lower than that of a backward clam—a clam, let us say, which had been dropped on its head when a baby—was at any rate ornamental.

This Cyril Phipps unquestionably was, and as for the slur on his intelligence, he would have been the first to agree that he had never been one of those brainy birds whose heads bulge out at the back. Some birds bulged and some birds didn't, you had to face it, he would have said, and he was one of the birds who didn't. At Eton everyone had called him Barmy. At Oxford everyone had called him Barmy. And even in the Drones Club, a place where the level of intellect is not high, it was as Barmy that he was habitually addressed. And when you looked at him, you felt how right and inevitable this was. The *mot juste*, you said to yourself.

It was not easy for Mr. Anderson to smile sunnily, but he forced his unaccustomed lips into something as nearly resembling a sunny smile as he could manage. It started to slide away as he recalled that this was the young man who had alluded to him as a priceless old stinker, but he grabbed it and put it back again. He was resolved to scatter sweetness and light, if it choked him.

"Come in, Phipps, come in," he cried effusively. "I hear you have a headache this morning. Too bad, too bad. You must take the day off. Sit down, Phipps, sit down. I want to have a little talk with you, my dear fellow."

Barmy sat down. It is doubtful if his legs would have supported him much longer. This effervescent cordiality, so different from what he had been expecting, had unmanned him. Thinking shudderingly of last night's dark doings, he had anticipated from the man up top something rather outstanding in the way of pique at their next meeting. He had not actually been present at the testing of the atom bomb at Bikini, but he had read about it, and something along these lines was what he had been envisaging in his mind's eye.

For consider the facts. After two years of unremitting respectfulness, two years of 'Yes, Mr. Anderson', 'Right ho, Mr. Anderson', 'Absolutely, Mr. Anderson' and 'Oh, rather, Mr. Anderson', he had so lapsed from his high standard of obsequious correctness as not only to break in on the other's sacred slumbers but actually to load him up with frogs, a reptile of which he had no reason to suppose that his overlord was fond. 'How art thou fallen from heaven, O Lucifer, son of the morning?' he had pictured Mr. Anderson saying. Among other things.

And now this breath-taking geniality. It was enough to remove the stuffing from a stronger man than Cyril Phipps.

"Cigarette, my boy?" said Mr. Anderson after a brief interval of silence, during which he was regretting that the latter's extraordinary wealth made it impossible for him to hurl at Barmy's head the silver presentation inkpot on his desk, to teach him not to let his lower jaw droop like that.

"Oh, thanks, right ho, thanks," said Barmy, accepting the peace pipe. His was one of those simple natures which respond readily to kindness, and he was beginning to feel at his ease again. He stopped fiddling with his Drones Club tie, his habit when perturbed, and prepared to be chatty. He saw now that he had been mistaken in supposing that his employer had sent for him in order to disembowel him with his bare hands. The way the interview was shaping, it looked more as though Mr. Anderson, feeling a little lonely, as we all do at times, and longing for somebody to pep him up, had said to himself, after running through the roster of his acquaintances, 'Phipps! That's the chap! Always merry and bright, always a fountain of entertaining small talk, I'll have Phipps up and get a laugh or two. Say what you will, there's nobody like good old Phipps.'

"A drink?" said Mr. Anderson, still coming through strongly with the sweetness and light.

Barmy shuddered a little.

"No, thanks frightfully," he said. A young man with a weakish head cannot revel in the grand Hollywood manner with someone like Mervyn Potter without feeling the effects next day, and he would have preferred not to have the word 'drink' mentioned in his presence. True, whoever it was who had been driving white-hot spikes into his skull had momentarily desisted from his activities, but he had still a long way to go before he could think of alcoholic refreshment without wincing.

"Then let's get down to it," said Mr. Anderson, who did not believe in beating about bushes. "Potter tells me you've come into money."

"Yes, sir."

"A great deal of money."

"Yes, sir. My grandfather on the mother's side. He ceased to tick over last Wednesday."

"Too bad."

"Yes, sir."

"Still, all flesh is grass."

"Yes, sir."

"We're here today and gone tomorrow, as the fellow said. Was your grandfather American?"

"Yes, sir. Oh, rather. Specifically American. His name was P. Middlemass Poskitt, and after—or while—making the dickens of a packet selling cut-out paper patterns, though why there should be any money in that is more than I can tell you, he took time off to have issue two daughters, Emerald and Ruby. Emerald married my Uncle Theodore, a thing I wouldn't have done myself on a bet, he being a sort of human snapping turtle, well known throughout England as the Curse of the Eastern Counties."

"That would be the Lord Binghampton I know?"

"That's right. I'd forgotten he was a pal of yours. Charming chap, I expect, when relaxing with the boys. I never saw that side of him. To me, from early childhood, he was always like one of those Human Fiends you get in the mystery stories. He could have stepped straight into an Edgar Wallace novel, and no questions asked."

"Maybe his bark was worse than his bite."

"Very possibly, though I cannot make any authoritative pronouncement, the old relative never having actually bitten me. I don't say he hasn't come close to it on occasion, but so far

I have always escaped unscathed. But I was telling you something, wasn't I?"

"You were saying that your grandfather had two daughters."

"Ah, yes. Well, the other one, Ruby, married my father and had issue one son. In a nutshell, me. You know, it's a rummy thing," said Barmy, who had recovered all his native chattiness and was looking on J. G. Anderson by this time as quite an old friend, "I had never for a moment expected to click. I hadn't so much as set eyes on this grandfather since I was a kind of fourteen in knickerbockers and pimples, and he gave no sign of being aware of my existence. I doubt if a bookie would have chalked me up on the slate as anything better than a thirty-to-one shot. It just shows you, doesn't it? Makes you think a bit, what?"

Mr. Anderson was wishing that his young guest would stop talking and give him an opportunity of getting down to business, but these big moneyed men have to be humoured, so he agreed that it made you think a bit.

"And I'll tell you another rummy thing," said Barmy, now the life and soul of the party. "Do you believe in what-d'you-call-its?"

"Eh?"

"Fortune-tellers."

"Oh, fortune-tellers? No, I do not."

"Then you're a chump of the first water, my dear old hotel proprietor, if you'll excuse me saying so. They're amazing birds. Just before I left England, I got lugged into attending a charity bazaar down Wimbledon way, and there was a fortune-teller there, operating in a tent, and as my shoes were a bit tight and the only prospect of taking the weight off my feet seemed to be to go and get five bobs' worth of this Gypsy Sybil, as she called herself, I filtered into the tent, and there she was, ensconced at a table with a crystal ball in front of her. I sank into the customers' chair, glad to rest the old dogs, and she scooped in my five bob, spat on her hands and snapped into action. Are you listening to any of this?"

Mr. Anderson said he was all ears, which, as a matter of fact, was very nearly true.

"Well, I won't be long. I'm coming to the nub. This Gypsy Sybil, having peered into the crystal ball, told me I had a rare spiritual nature and great personal charm, though people meeting me for the first time were apt not to appreciate me to the full because I had such deep reserves and hidden depths. She then touched on the future, and this is where I got my full five bobs' worth. She said I was about to take a long journey and was going to meet a fair girl and have a spot of trouble from a dark man and—mark this—I was going to get pots of money. Well, I've taken the long journey and I've got the pots of money, so now what ho for the fair girl, what?"

Mr. Anderson, with a strong effort of the will, forced himself to say "Exactly".

"I'm not worrying so much about the dark man, though I suppose dark men can make themselves pretty unpleasant if you stir them up, but I do want to meet that fair girl. Nothing was actually stated in set terms, but the Gypsy Sybil rather hinted that she would be all over me. Fling herself into my arms and say 'My mate!', and all that sort of thing. Well, nothing could fit in better with my plans, for if there's one thing one wants, it's fair girls flinging themselves into your arms and saying 'My mate!'. Or don't you think so?"

Mr. Anderson, who would have called the police if a fair girl had made a single step in his direction, said he certainly did, and, taking advantage of the fact that his young friend had fallen into a reverie and was gazing into space in a starry-eyed manner, changed the subject and turned the conversation to business.

"Tell me," he said. "What are you planning to do with all this money of yours?"

Barmy came to himself with a start. He gently removed the fair girl, who had been sitting on his lap, curling his hair with her fingers.

"Eh? My money? Oh, you mean my money. What am I going to do with it? Well, really, dash it, I don't quite know."

"I do," said Mr. Anderson jovially. "You're going to buy the Washington."

"The Washington?" he said. His mind was not at its nimblest this morning.

"That's right."

"The Washington Hotel?"

For an instant it seemed as though Mr. Anderson were about to forget sweetness and light and say that he had not been alluding to the Washington Monument, you mutton-headed half-wit, and go on to speak forcefully of dumb bricks with about as much quickness in the uptake as a frog. And talking of frogs . . .

The weakness passed. He reassembled the sunny smile,

fastening it painfully on his face once more as if with pins.

"The Washington Hotel. You've been working there long enough to know it's a gold mine. Most people would say I was a fool to let it go, but here's how it is. I want to spend my winters down South, and I'm planning to buy a hotel in Florida. Palm Beach or Miami or wherever it may be. Before I can do that, I've got to get rid of the Washington, and there's no one I'd rather have it than you. Young fellow I've trained myself. Now naturally," said Mr. Anderson, observing that the party of the second part was still looking like a ventriloquist's dummy and realizing that something in the nature of an interval would have to elapse before his mind, using that word loosely, would be able to absorb the salient points of the scheme, "I don't expect you to decide a thing like this offhand. Go away and think it over, and then come back and we'll have another talk."

★ 3 ★

As Barmy left the presence and made for the open air, his mind was in a whirl and there was a fever in his blood. Mr. Anderson's proposition had enlarged his horizon and opened up new vistas before him. For the first time since he had received the lawyer's letter informing him of his novel affluence, he was feeling the surge of power which great riches bring with them.

Until now, though his headache had been too painful to allow him to give much thought to it, he had supposed that all you could do with any money that came your way was to bung it into safe income-bearing securities and return to position one, continuing as before to sit behind a desk and give patrons their keys and letters. He had long realized that he was not a man of exceptional gifts, being rather one of the multitude who are dashed lucky to land a job of any kind and priceless asses if they do not stick to that job like glue. Fate had made him a desk clerk, and a desk clerk he must continue to be.

But this, Mr. Anderson had made him see, was a tame policy, unworthy of a man of enterprise. By making that amazing proposal, J. G. Anderson had removed the scales from his eyes, and with this clearer vision had come ambition and the desire to escape from the humdrum round and live the larger life, like Mervyn Potter. Barmy had not seen very much of Mervyn Potter since that first meeting in London, but he had seen enough to be convinced that when it came to leading the larger life, he had few equals.

It was as he came out on to the gravel sweep outside the main entrance to the hotel that he heard his name called and, looking up, saw Mervyn Potter. The motion picture star was seated at the wheel of his car, distributing a few autographs to members of his public.

"Hello, there," he said, as Barmy came up. "How's the head?"

"Eh? Oh, much better, thanks. Agony considerably abated."

23

"I am rejoiced to hear it. But the mere absence of a headache is not enough to account for the rapt expression that was on your face as you emerged from the hotel. You looked like the Soul's Awakening. Why were you going around with rapt expressions on your face, Phipps, old friend?"

"I was doing a spot of thinking."

"About what?"

Barmy was only too happy to confine in this knowledgeable man. The one thing he had been subconsciously longing for was a sympathetic adviser in whose judgment he could trust. He was not aware that America was full of broken men who had asked Mervyn Potter for advice and taken it. He poured forth the story of J. G. Anderson's proposal, and Mervyn Potter simply sneered at the idea of buying the Hotel Washington of Bessemer, Ohio.

"Buy his hotel?" said Mervyn Potter.

"That's what he suggested."

"You don't want to buy any ruddy hotels."

"Don't I?"

"Certainly not. It would be madness. Just chucking your money away. Men who own hotels always wind up in the bread line with holes in their socks. It's the overhead that does them in. The most bottomless purse cannot stand the constant drain of having to buy fresh supplies of soap and new towels, to replace those taken away by guests in their suitcases. You would be astounded, Phipps, if I told you how much soap and how many towels are pinched annually from hotels. I myself have pinched soap and towels from practically every hotel from the rockbound coast of Massachusetts to the alligator-haunted Everglades of Florida, and I am not one of the really big operators. No, no, we must think of something better than a hotel. I don't want to be strolling through the Bowery some night and see a ragged form asleep in the gutter and recognize it with a visible start as that of my old friend Phipps. I'll tell you what I'd do, if I were as rich as you."

This surprised Barmy.

"Aren't you?"

"Of course I'm not. We Hollywood hams are not rich men, Phipps. We think we are for a few happy moments when we are counting the contents of the envelope on pay day, and then we feel a tap on our shoulder; there, standing beside us waiting to twist our arm, is a gentleman with whiskers who takes it all off us, skinning us to the bone."

"Taxes, you mean?"

Mervyn Potter winced.

"Don't mention that word, Phipps. Without wishing to wound, you have touched an exposed, nerve. Yes, taxes, if you must have it."

"I suppose they're pretty big."

"Supercolossal. And then there are all the incidental expenses of life in the golden West. Polo ponies, yachts, swimming pools, wives . . . it all mounts up. I have been forced to abandon Hollywood for the time being in order to make my economies. In New York, with its comparative absence of temptations to extravagance, I may be able to put by a little nest egg. I am appearing shortly in a play on Broadway."

"Yes, somebody told me that. It's bound to be a success."

"Naturally."

"I mean to say, you have a terrific following, haven't you?"

"Enormous. And practically all women. The ladies love me, Phipps, and who are we to blame them, poor saps?"

"I suppose that's what counts in the theatre?"

"It's the only thing that counts. Get the women, and it's in the bag. There won't be an empty seat in the house or a dry eye or any of the usual things. Which brings me back to what I was about to say just now. It's obvious what you must do with your wealth. You must put it into this play of mine. I like you, Phipps, and I want to see you doubling—nay, trebling—your vast fortune, so that in the years to come, when my hair is grey and the profile marred by a couple of extra chins, I shall be able to touch you for the means of livelihood. Lehmac Productions, Incorporated, are running the venture, if you can call such a cast-iron certainty a venture, and I am sure Lehman would be delighted to sell you a slice. Go to New York and see him. You'll like being a manager. Nothing to it but sit back and watch the other fellows work and draw your handsome profits. The ideal life, if you ask me. So trot along and tell Anderson the deal is off, because you have decided to invest your millions in the drama. And now," said Mervyn Potter, "I must leave you. I am going to Skeewassett to purchase as much of a gent's nobby outfit as I can find there. Good-bye, Phipps. We shall meet at Philippi.

My fiancée and I are flying to New York after lunch, for rehearsals have already begun, and my place is by their side. By the time I see you again, I shall expect to find you a full-blown manager. I shall have to touch my hat to you and call you Sir."

And having signed a few more autographs for a few more members of his public who had happened to wander by, Mervyn Potter drove off, waving a cheery hand.

For some moments after he had disappeared, Barmy stood motionless on the gravel, weighing pros and cons. Like Mr. Anderson, Mervyn Potter had enlarged his horizon and opened up new vistas, and he had unquestionably been conscious during the motion picture star's harangue of a quick upsurge of the spirit of adventure. But gradually this began to ebb.

After all, he reasoned, the Washington was his home. It was a safe haven, and would he not be rash in the last degree to leave it for uncharted seas? He decided that he would. As he made his way to Mr. Anderson's office, he was once more feeling strongly in favour of closing with his employer's offer. Mervyn Potter's gloomy estimate of the hotel business had shaken him for a while, but now Reason was returning to its throne.

Mervyn Potter, it seemed to him, had got his facts twisted. Barmy had been working for J. G. Anderson long enough to know that he was an extremely prosperous old gentleman. Even allowing for losses on soap and towels, it was obvious to one who had held the post as desk clerk in his caravanserai for two years that J. G. Anderson found the pickings good. He ate expensively, dressed expensively, bought expensive automobiles and smoked dollar cigars. There was no room for question that the man was on velvet and that anyone who succeeded him as owner of the Hotel Washington would be on velvet, too.

Mr. Anderson was smoking a dollar cigar as Barmy entered the office. He looked up, beaming with all the old chumminess.

"Ah, Phipps. Back again?"

"Yes, sir."

"Feeling better?"

"Yes, sir."

"Good. Well, you've caught me just in time, my boy. I have to go to Skeewassett to see my lawyer. But I'll be able to give you a few figures before I start. These are for the year ending

December thirty-first last," said Mr. Anderson, and began to spout them like a geyser.

To Barmy they conveyed precisely nothing, but from the way his employer rolled them round his tongue as if they were vintage port he divined that they must be pretty hot, and his last doubts vanished. When Mr. Anderson, pausing and lowering the paper from which he was reading, said 'Well?' it was without hesitation that he replied 'Oh, rather. Absolutely'.

"Pretty good?" said Mr. Anderson.

"Dashed good," said Barmy.

"You want to buy the Washington?"

"Oh, definitely."

"Then here's my proposition. You can have it for a hundred thousand."

There came over Barmy that sensation of having been suddenly slapped in the face with a wet towel which is so unpleasant. He also felt as if he had been kicked in the stomach by a more than usually sinewy army mule. He gasped, gurgled, tottered and stood fingering his Drones Club tie.

"A hundred thousand?"

"A hundred thousand."

"But I say, dash it, I haven't got a hundred thousand."

"How much have you got?"

"Twenty-two thousand, eighteen cents."

Mr. Anderson quivered in every limb. He ceased to beam. The love feast was over. The look which he was now directing at his desk clerk was one of those hard, reproachful looks which hotel proprietors anxious to unload a portion of their holdings direct at desk clerks who have led them on, played the fool with them, wasted their time and raised their hopes only to dash them to the ground. Not even when accepting that frog at his hands at three o'clock in the morning had J. G. Anderson felt so keen a distaste for his young subordinate.

"Twenty-two thousand?" he said hoarsely.

"And eighteen cents. You see," explained Barmy, "my Uncle Theodore of course copped the jackpot. Most of the stuff in the old oak chest went to him. After all, he was the old boy's son-in-law and had always clustered round him pretty assiduously, paying annual visits to New York to slap him on the back and say 'What ho', whereas I——"

Mr. Anderson had been counting slowly.

"Ten!" he said, having arrived at that figure. Then, speaking with a curious mildness, "Phipps," he said.

"Hullo?"

"You busy?"

"Oh no, rather not."

"Then I wish you would do something for me."

With a quick gesture Mr. Anderson directed Barmy's attention to the open window. It afforded an excellent view of Lake Skeewassett.

"It won't take you long. You see that lake?"

Barmy said he saw that lake.

"Well, I want you to get a boat and go out on that lake. Row out about two hundred yards from the shore. The water is deep there?"

"Oh, rather. Very deep."

"Good. Then row out about two hundred yards from the shore, and when you're there tie something heavy around your damned neck and jump in and drown yourself. Good morning," said Mr. Anderson, and left the room. He was already late for his appointment with his lawyer.

Barmy drew himself up. A mild young man normally, there had been something in Mr. Anderson's words—his tone, possibly —which had offended him. When the other suddenly reappeared in the doorway, his eyes did not actually flash, for they were the sort of eyes which do not flash readily, but his manner was cold.

"Something I forgot to say," said Mr. Anderson. "You're fired. If I see you here again, I'll kill you, if I have to do it with a corkscrew."

Barmy laughed raspingly. A strange light had come into his eyes. His mind was made up. He had decided to follow Mervyn Potter's admirable advice and do the drama a bit of good. He wondered how he could ever have been attracted by the silly idea of becoming a hotel proprietor when this other glittering path lay open before him.

"I am, am I?" he said. "Fired, eh? Well, it may interest you to learn, you blighted old object, that if you hadn't buzzed off like a scalded cat, I was just about to tender my resignation as of even date. If you want to know what I'm going to do——"

"I don't."

"I'm going to be a manager."

"Hotel manager?"

"Theatrical manager. I'm going into show business."

"God help it!" said Mr. Anderson, and disappeared again, this time permanently.

★ 4 ★

IT was on a Monday that this painful scene had taken place, and Barmy, feeling correctly that there was nothing to keep him, left Skeewassett by the evening train, arriving in New York on the Tuesday morning in time for a latish breakfast at the hotel off Madison Avenue which had been his first home when he had come to America two years ago.

The journey, like all American train journeys, had been bumpy, leaving him limp and jaded, and it was not until he had slept through the afternoon and taken a refreshing shower that he felt equal to sauntering out and seeing the sights.

When he did so, one of the first sights he saw was Mervyn Potter. The motion picture star was standing at the corner of Madison Avenue and Sixty-Fifth Street giving his autograph to a small girl in pigtails.

"Ah, Phipps," he said cordially, as Barmy approached. "You do pop up, don't you? I believe I mentioned to you in the course of a recent conversation that this was a beautiful world. What makes it so beautiful is that there is never any shortage of Phippses. Wherever you go—north, south, east or west—there you find Cyril Fotheringay-Phipps. I will be with you in a moment."

He finished inscribing his name in the grubby album, and the small child toddled away into the unknown. Mervyn Potter passed a weary hand over his forehead.

"One's public, Phipps, one's public!" he sighed. "A great strain, this continual coping with the incessant homage of the fans. Not that I mind my own fans so much. The human rats into whose malted milk shakes I feel an urge to slip a shot of some little-known Asiatic poison are the ones who ask me for my autograph under the mistaken impression that I am Gregory Peck. I believe genuine Gregory Pecks sell for forty cents on the black market, while I fetch only a quarter, and I resent the way the young reptiles gulp with ill-concealed chagrin when they see what they've got. But let us change a distasteful subject. So

30

here you are in New York. Ah, New York, New York! The centre
of the universe. I used to be the brightest jewel in its crown
before I went to Hollywood, and I hope to resume that position
when this play is running in a blaze of glory."

"I suppose you've been rehearsing?"

"All day. Another great strain. Rehearsals are dull work."

"Pretty ghastly, I imagine."

"Tedious to a degree. One has to be constantly on the alert
to find ways of alleviating the monotony. I think, however, that
I begin to see daylight. There was a fat gentleman there today
who slept soundly all through my big scenes. Tomorrow, if he
is there again and repeats his act, I shall give him a hot foot."

"What's that?"

Mervyn Potter was amazed.

"You mean you have been in America two years and don't
know what a hot foot is? Why, over here children learn to give
the hot foot in kindergarten. It is the first thing they are taught.
You take a simple match, you look about you till you see some
friend or acquaintance whose attention has been diverted else-
where, you insert the match between the sock and the side of
the shoe, light it and let Nature take its course. As simple as that.
We should have tried it on J. G. Anderson. How did you leave
dear old J.G., by the way? Did he hit the ceiling when you told
him you were not going to buy his termite-ridden hotel?"

"He did seem a bit stirred."

"I'll bet he was as mad as a wet hen. And you know how mad
hens are, when wet. Have you got in touch with Lehman yet?"

"I thought of ringing him up tomorrow."

"And tonight? What are your plans for tonight?"

"I don't think I have any."

"Excellent. Perhaps you would come and have a bite of dinner
with me?"

"I'd love it."

"My fiancée is going to a dance or some such rout or revel
out at King's Point, Long Island, where she resides, and your
jolly society is just what I need to cheer me up. We'll go to some
quiet restaurant. Look me up around eight at the Renfrew on
East Sixty-Sixth Street, where I have taken a modest apartment.
Don't dress. Oh, Phipps?"

"Hullo?"

"Have you had my autograph? No. It is a thing no young man

starting life ought to be without. Here you are. Wear it next your heart or sell it for a quarter, whichever course appeals to you. Au revoir, then, Phipps. At the Renfrew as the clocks are striking eight," said Mervyn Potter. "Give three quick rings and whistle the first few bars of 'The Star-Spangled Banner'."

He passed on with a benevolent nod, and Barmy resumed his walk, puffing happily at the cigar which he had bought at the hotel counter and enjoying the coolness which had crept into the air with the approach of evening. He looked forward with bright anticipation to tomorrow's interview with Mr. Lehman of Lehmac Productions. He was not quite sure at what hour theatrical managers liked to be called up and asked for an appointment, and wished that he had consulted Mervyn Potter on this point, but, allowing Mr. Lehman a reasonable time for lunch, he supposed that somewhere in the neighbourhood of two-thirty would be about it.

He also looked forward to tonight's dinner with Mervyn Potter, always such excellent company. If a passing thought of dangers of hobnobbing with that eccentric character flitted into his mind, he dismissed it. Even Mervyn Potter, he reflected, could scarcely introduce any novel variations into a quiet restaurant dinner. He had yet to realize that there was no social function into which the other could not introduce novel variations.

It was at this point in his saunter, just as he was thinking what a capital fellow Mervyn Potter was and what a capital fellow Mr. Lehman would doubtless prove to be, that he beheld something which brought him up with a round turn, the cigar frozen on his lips, his impressionable soul seething like a cistern struck by a thunderbolt.

"Oof!" he said, tottering.

What his eye had rested on was the back view of a girl in some sort of beige upholstery, who was standing looking into a shop window, and it was a back view which seemed to speak to his very depths. Back views, of course, are not every-thing, and he was aware that the prudent man reserves judgment until that crucial point in the proceedings when the subject turns round, nevertheless he stood stunned and goggling. He had that feeling, which comes to all of us at times, that a high spot in his life had been reached and that he was about to undergo some great spiritual experience.

With a vague thought that at a sacred moment like this a man

with any claim to the finer feelings ought not to be puffing a great,
fat, smelly cigar, he hurled the remains of his from him with a
passionate sweep of the hand, and having done so, stood petrified.

"Oh, my sainted aunt!" he ejaculated.

The girl, absorbed, did not hear the observation. She had
come all the way from Broadway to gaze at this shop window,
and she was not to be distracted by the mere mention of somebody's aunt, sainted or otherwise. She continued to press her
nose against the glass.

Eileen ('Dinty') Moore was one of those girls of the fifty to sixty
dollars a week class who do most of their big shopping through
windows. On fine evenings, when her day's work was done, it was
her practice to walk across town and indulge in an emotional orgy
among the Madison Avenue shops. The emporium in front of
which she was standing now was that of Noreen O'Hara, who
sells hats. And she was staring wistfully at a superb specimen
which looked like a fruit salad, wishing that she could afford a
spectacular number like that in place of her own modest lid, when
a finger touched her arm, a voice said 'I say' and, turning, she
saw that what had come into her life was a willowy young man
with hair the colour of creamery butter and an open, engaging
face.

"I say," he said.

"Yes?" said Dinty.

She spoke with a certain cold austerity, and a hard glaze had
formed itself over her attractive eyes. She disliked wolves, and
though this young man did not look like one, she had been earning
her living in New York long enough to know that many wolves,
and not the least predatory of them, go about in sheep's clothing,
deceiving the eye with open, engaging faces.

Her voice, accordingly, was chilly and packed with menace,
and the chill and the menace would have been more noticeable
than they were, but for the fact that Barmy's open, engaging
face had aroused the maternal instinct in her. It has been mentioned that this was frequently the effect it had on women. Even
while eyeing him with the same hard intentness with which Jack
Dempsey used to regard his opponents in the ring, she was
conscious of a strong impulse to stroke his head.

Had she done so, it would have been all right with Barmy.
Seeing her steadily and seeing her whole, he felt no slackening
off of the turmoil in the depths of his being. It had, indeed, risen

to a new high. For, sensational though the back view had been, the front view topped it. In spades. A single rapid glance had been enough to tell Barmy that of all the girls he had ever set eyes on this was the Girl Supreme. He had never fallen in love at first sight with such wholeheartedness before, not even on the occasion, three years ago, when he had come into the grocer's shop at Bridmouth-on-Sea with Catsmeat Potter-Pirbright and seen Angelica Briscoe of the Vicarage, Maiden Eggesford, buying five ounces of streaky bacon.

The warmth of his emotion would have surprised many of Dinty's circle, her employer for one. If you had asked him for a word portrait of his secretary, he would have told you that there was nothing very special about her. Just an ordinary kid, he would have said, fairly pretty, blue eyes, fair hair, much the same as all the other kids you saw around, nothing much about her one way or the other. But to Barmy she seemed like some ethereal spirit possessed of everything that it takes. Gazing at her, he marvelled that there could ever have been a time when he had supposed Angelica Briscoe, of the Vicarage, Maiden Eggesford, to be what the doctor had ordered. This girl, it seemed to him, began where Angelica Briscoe left off. He took off his hat to the Gypsy Sybil. This, he felt, was a fair girl to end all fair girls.

If there was any possible criticism that he could have made of her façade, it would have been that he could have done with a shade less stoniness in the eyes. But even though stony, they dazzled him. He was fascinated by the way her nose turned up at the tip, and if ever a mouth like hers had been issued to any other girl, the fact had not been drawn to his attention.

It was a mouth, indeed, capable of smiling delightfully and with a friendly warmth, but at the moment the lips were set in a hard, straight line, and they scarcely parted as she put her question once more.

"Yes?" said Dinty. "And what can I do for you, brother? Do you want to sell me the Brooklyn Bridge?"

Barmy saw that there had been a misapprehension. He did not own the Brooklyn Bridge. He mentioned this.

"No?" said Dinty. "What do you own . . . besides a lot of nerve?"

A sudden uncomfortable thought struck Barmy. He was not exceptionally intuitive, but he could reason and deduce.

"I say, you aren't shirty because I spoke to you?"

" A little displeased."

"Oh, my aunt, I'm frightfully sorry. I wouldn't have done it, but a rather serious situation has arisen and I thought I ought to clarify it."

"Start clarifying."

Barmy marshalled his thoughts, as well as his emotion would let him.

"Well, it's this way—I'm staying at a hotel round the corner——"

"Nice place?"

"Oh, rather."

"Comfortable there?"

"Oh, rather."

"Good. It makes me very happy to know that. Yes? You were saying?"

"Well, I was coming out for a stroll, and I bought a cigar at the hotel counter——"

"Good cigar?"

"Oh, very."

"Fine. Proceed. When do we get the big situation?"

"I'm just coming to it. You see, I was smoking this cigar, and I chucked it away with a careless gesture——"

"Like the fellow who shot an arrow into the air. Did you ever meet him? It fell to earth, he knew not where."

"It did, eh? Yes, one can see how that might be so. But between that arrow and my cigar there is a substantial difference, because my cigar didn't fall to earth, not by a jugful. It fell on your hat."

He had arrested her attention. His story had gripped her.

"My hat!"

"That's right. And I have a growing suspicion that it's on fire."

"You mean that at any moment I may be going up in flames?"

"I wouldn't be surprised."

"Why couldn't you have told me that at once?"

"I was sort of leading up to it."

"You needn't have tried to break it gently. Girls like to know these things. Have a look," said Dinty, bending down.

Barmy removed the cigar, flung it aside, hit a passing pedestrian, said 'Oh, sorry' and issued his bulletin.

"Well, you seem to have stopped smouldering——"

"That's good."

"——but I'm afraid the old lid isn't what it used to be. Pretty much of a devastated area, I fear." His eye fell on Noreen O'Hara's shop window, and inspiration came to him. "I say, you must let me buy you another."

"Oh, no, that's all right. Don't bother."

"What do you mean, don't bother? I can't go about the place ruining people's hats and not replacing them. I'll buy you a dozen, if you like."

"Who are you? The Great Gatsby?"

"Gatsby? No. My name's——"

"I mean, are you a millionaire?"

"Well, I've got quite a bit of the stuff. My grandfather on the mother's side conked out recently, respected by all, and left me a considerable packet."

"I see. Well, in that case, all right, and thanks a lot. But a cheap one."

"Cheap be blowed," said Barmy. "The best the place can supply."

He escorted her masterfully into Noreen O'Hara's.

Noreen O'Hara proved a willing and sympathetic collaborator. Barmy's statement that the lady required a hat brought her up on her toes in an instant, and when he added that in the matter of price the sky might be regarded as the limit, it seemed to arouse all that was best in her. She bustled about, exhibiting specimen after specimen, but it was the one that looked like a fruit salad that received Dinty's vote. She came out with it poised on her head, and Barmy quivered to the soles of his suède shoes as he gazed at it. He had not supposed that it would have been possible to enhance her radiant beauty, but the fruit salad did it by as much as twenty per cent.

"Well, thank you again ever so much," she said. "If you knew how I hated that old hat of mine, and I thought I would have to make it last for ever. Gosh, I feel like the girl who got a fur coat by standing outside Bergdorf Goodman's and saying 'Brrrrh!'. Not my own, but I'm glad it went so well," said Dinty, observing that her companion was chuckling with some heartiness.

Barmy explained the cause of his mirth.

"I was just laughing because of a rather odd coincidence. It suddenly occurred to me that this is the second time in two days that I've got mixed up in a fire."

"That tickled you?"

"It did a bit."

"You must be as easily amused as a studio audience. What happened the other time?"

"I rescued a chap from a burning bungalow. Snatched him from the flames, as you might say."

"And now you've snatched me from the flames. You want to watch yourself. You're getting into a rut. Well, I'll have to be moving along."

"Oh, I say, must you?"

"I've got a date miles away uptown."

"Oh, dash it. All right, I'll hail you a cab."

"You millionaires! I don't take cabs. I take buses."

She leaped lightly into the one which had just pulled up at the kerb and, as it moved away, Barmy stood gaping after it, his lower jaw drooping in the manner which had so often aroused the fiend that slept in J. G. Anderson. It had just occurred to him that, having met his fair girl, precisely as predicted by the Gypsy Sybil, he had omitted to inform himself of her name, address and telephone number. And now she was gone, gone like the wind, and he would never see her again. They were ships that pass in the night, he was thinking. Just a couple of ruddy ships that pass in the bally night.

Madison Avenue swam before his eyes. He had never seen a more flickering thoroughfare.

★ 5 ★

IT was a sombre, Byronic Barmy, a Barmy with a heart bowed
down with weight of woe and a soul with blisters on it, who at
eight o'clock that night presented himself at the door of Mervyn
Potter's apartment. The more he brooded on the afternoon's
happenings, the more he found himself resenting Fate's distorted
sense of humour. By dangling the only girl in the world before
his eyes and then snatching her away just when it seemed possible
that business might result, Fate, he considered, had played a low
practical joke on him. He could appreciate now how that swan
on the lake of Binghampton Hall must have felt, that time when,
a boy of twelve, incapable of understanding the other fellow's
point of view, he had offered it a piece of Bath bun tied to a
string, dexterously jerking it out of reach every time the bird
snapped at it. It had made the swan as sick as mud, he recalled,
and he had laughed consumedly, but, himself the victim of a
similar pleasantry, though of course on the spiritual plane, he
blushed to think that he could have been guilty of such sharp
practice.

"Ah, well," he said to himself, or words to that effect, and
pressed the Potter doorbell. Footsteps sounded, the door opened,
and he was immediately pinned by the right trouser leg by a
large saffron-coloured dog which had come oozing silently over
the threshold.

"Ouch!" he cried, a good deal stirred and momentarily
forgetting his frustrated love life.

Mervyn Potter, who followed in the animal's wake, greeted
him cordially. He had a glass full of amber liquid in his hand,
and inhaled a draught from this.

"Hello there," he said. "Fotheringay-Phipps, is it not?"

"That's right."

"The Fotheringay-Phipps there has been so much talk about?
The Fotheringay-Phipps? Well, well, well," said Mervyn Potter,
"this is the proudest day of my life. Come on in and have a drink."

38

"I'd love to," said Barmy, "only there seems to be a dog of sorts attached to my leg."

Mervyn Potter narrowed his gaze.

"You're perfectly right. My Tanganyika lion dog, Tulip. You're a very quick observer, Phipps. Many fellows wouldn't have noticed that."

Barmy, as he followed his host into the sitting-room, began to find a certain uneasiness mingling with his spiritual anguish. It was plain to him that the other, fatigued no doubt after a long day's rehearsal, had yielded to the dictates of his lower self and for some considerable time must have been mopping up the stuff like a vacuum cleaner. If not actually ossified, he was indubitably plastered, and Barmy could only hope that he would not eventually reach the truculent stage. A bimbo as large and muscular as Mervyn Potter was not at all the sort of bimbo you wanted to have getting truculent around you.

At present he was all amiability. He pressed refreshment on Barmy, absorbed a considerable quantity himself and spoke interestingly of life in Hollywood, telling many a diverting anecdote about fellow stars of his and studio executives he had met.

"You ever been cornered by a wounded studio executive, Phipps? No? It's an experience every young man ought to have. Broadens the mind and helps to form the character. How well I remember the day when I was wandering through the jungle on the Metro-Goldwyn lot and Louis B. Mayer suddenly sprang out at me from the undergrowth. He had somehow managed to escape from the office where they kept him, and I could see from his glaring eyes and slavering jaws that he had already tasted blood. Fortunately I had my elephant gun and my trusty native bearer with me. . . ." Mervyn Potter's attention seemed to wander. "Well, good night, all," he said, and fell asleep.

Barmy ventured to touch him on the arm.

"I say!"

Mervyn Potter opened his eyes.

"I have the skin hanging on my wall at Beverly Hills," he said, concluding his narrative.

"I say!"

"Yes, Phipps?"

"It's getting pretty late. Don't you think we might go and have dinner?"

Mervyn Potter stared. "Have *dinner?* You don't want any dinner."

"Yes, I do."

"No, you don't. Sit down!" bellowed Mervyn Potter in a voice of thunder.

Barmy sat down. It was clear that his host had now reached that truculent stage which he had hoped might have been avoided, and he found himself wishing that he had got mixed up with one of the rather smaller motion picture stars.

"Dinner!" said Mervyn Potter, and adding the word 'Faugh!', closed his eyes and fell once more into a refreshing sleep.

From the way he had said 'Dinner! Faugh!', Barmy could see that Mervyn Potter did not think much of the meal, but he could not share the other's contemptuous detachment. He had eaten nothing since his latish breakfast, and with every moment that passed was becoming more conscious of the need for nourishment. His stomach had begun to make low, querulous noises, and it seemed to him that it would be an excellent idea to take advantage of his companion's slumber to creep out and fortify himself. If a chap asks you to dinner, he reasoned, you naturally stick around till he gives the signal for putting on the nosebag, but once it has become obvious that mine host has no intention of giving such a signal and that, as far as he is concerned, no calories may be expected, you can consider yourself at liberty to slide out and forage on your own. Emily Post, he was sure, would endorse this view.

He rose, accordingly, poising himself for flight, and instantaneously the room became filled with a curious gargling sound, as if some giant were using mouth-wash in the vicinity. Between himself and the door the dog Tulip was standing with a wealth of meaning in his eyes. The most amateur physiognomist would have discerned that there stood a dog prompt on all occasions to deal with funny business. And that Barmy's desire to leave the premises fell in his opinion into this category was only too sickeningly evident.

Barmy attempted to find a formula.

"Nice doggie," he said. "Won't oo let me pass?"

The animal gave a quick impressionist imitation of a mad bloodhound with a fishbone in its throat.

"Oh, all right," said Barmy, a little stiffly. "I merely asked."

The hour now was about eight-forty-five. At a quarter past

eleven Mervyn Potter sat up and stretched himself. He seemed fresh and rested.

"Nothing like a bit of sleep," he said, reaching for the decanter and taking an aperitif. "Knits up the ravelled sleeve of care, I often say. And how's my old Phippsy?"

"I'm all right," said Barmy, though it was a loose interpretation of the facts.

"You managed to amuse yourself while I was having my nap? I was sure you would. No doubt you and Tulip exchanged views on this and that? A fine dog, is he not?"

"Oh, rather. Very fine. But is he safe?"

"Perfectly, I should imagine. Nobody would be ass enough to try to attack Tulip. His strength is as the strength of ten, because his heart is pure. Well, Phipps, the night is drawing on. Shall we go out and see what the town has to offer? They tell me the cabaret at the Piazza is worth a visit."

"That would be fine."

"Then let's go. Come on, Tulip."

"But you can't take a dog to the Piazza."

A dangerous look came into Mervyn Potter's face. His eyes narrowed, as if he had been the hero of a Western film confronted with cattle rustlers. Nothing annoys the man of haughty spirit more than having people dictating to him.

"Who says I can't take a dog to the Piazza? Did you?" he said, eyeing Barmy keenly.

"No, no."

"I could have sworn I heard somebody say it," said Mervyn Potter, puzzled. "Some trick of the acoustics, no doubt. Come along, Phipps. Fall in, Tulip. Next stop, the Piazza."

Revellers in considerable numbers had assembled to watch the cabaret at the Piazza Hotel, and the Champagne Room, where it broke loose twice nightly, was congested, but by force of personality Mervyn Potter succeeded in securing a table at the edge of the dancing floor. The dog Tulip, after a certain amount of rather acrimonious argument, had been accommodated with a shakedown in the cloak-room. The waiter brought the menu, and Barmy's stomach caught Barmy's eye in a congratulatory sort of way, like a stomach seeing the approach of the happy ending.

Mervyn Potter waved the man aside.

"Nothing to eat," he said. "Just a bottle of champagne."

Barmy felt his stomach spring to its feet with raised eyebrows.

"I say!" he bleated. "I could do with a few kidneys or a couple of steaks or something."

"No, you couldn't. Kidneys? Steaks? After that enormous dinner? You mustn't make a god of your stomach, Phipps," said Mervyn Potter rebukingly. "Put it down out of my friend's reach," he added, as the waiter arrived with the champagne. "A nice chap," he explained, taking the man into his confidence with the genial charm which was so characteristic of him, "but one of those fellows who never know when to stop. He's been swilling it down since breakfast. One glass, Phipps, just to be sociable, but no more."

"But, I say——"

That dangerous look came into Mervyn Potter's face again.

"Not going to start an argument, are you, Phipps?"

"No, no."

"Good," said Mervyn Potter, and dozed off.

It seemed to Barmy that the time had come to call it a day. He could see no pleasure or profit resulting from the continued society of this plastered idol of the silver screen. There came upon him an urge to get away from it all.

He drew back a leg preparatory to rising, and an unseen something gripped it in strong teeth. Reckless of the possibility that the other might wake up cross, he shook his host by the arm.

"Yes?" said Mervyn Potter, stirring in his sleep. "Oh, hullo, Phipps. I was hoping I'd run into you. Is that Fotheringay sitting at your side? How are you, Fotheringay? Listen, you two, I've just remembered something that may be useful to you. When a studio executive charges you, look to the left but leap to the right. This baffles the simple creature."

Barmy thanked him, and said that he would make a note of it.

"Changing the subject for a moment," he said, "that dog of yours is under the table. He's got me by the leg."

Mervyn Potter raised the cloth and verified the statement.

"You're perfectly correct, Phipps. So he has. Hi ya, Tulip."

He resumed his slumbers.

It was some faint relief to Barmy that the cabaret now began. He had been feeling the need of something to take him out of himself. Watching it, he was able to a certain extent to ignore the peevish complaints his stomach persisted in making. Mervyn Potter continued to sleep.

But not for long. In every cabaret entertainment there is included a concerted number in the course of which the personnel of the ensemble start throwing things at the customers, and those responsible for the arrangement of the programme at the Piazza had not omitted this item. A few minutes later a cottonwool snowball, an indispensable adjunct to the concerted number "Winter Time", struck Mervyn Potter on one of his closed eyes. As he opened it, another struck him on the tip of the nose. When chorus girls see a client asleep at a ringside table, they do not waste their ammunition on more wakeful patrons.

The song 'We don't want to fight, but by Jingo if we do!' might have been written by its author specially with someone like Mervyn Potter in mind. Mervyn Potter was a man who, if you left him alone, would leave you alone. He was all for peace in our time. But anybody who supposed him lacking in pride and spirit was vastly mistaken.

"This can't go on," he said quietly, and those who knew Mervyn Potter best could have told you that he was never more to be feared than when he spoke in that grim undertone.

He raised the tablecloth. A saffron head peered out inquiringly. Mervyn Potter waved a hand in the direction of the personnel of the ensemble, who were now doing something mysterious with snow-shoes.

"Sic 'em, Tulip," he said.

6

Barmy rose from the gutter outside the Piazza Hotel and dizzily adjusted his tie. He could not recall exactly how he had got there, but he remembered the order in which their little party had struck the pavement. First himself, then Mervyn Potter, and finally Tulip, who had sailed through the air and hit him between the shoulder-blades. Looking about him now, he saw his two companions respectively dusting trousers and barking at the management. Neither seemed in any way disconcerted by what had occurred. Mervyn Potter in particular appeared to be in radiant spirits. That slight irritability which had occasionally been noticeable in his manner of late had entirely gone.

"And what now, Phipps?" he said cheerily.

"Bed?" suggested Barmy.

Mervyn Potter seemed astounded.

"Bed? At this time? The shank of the evening? No, Phipps, I think we can do better than that. The neighbourhood in which we are is so congested with cabarets that the pleasure-seeker has an almost illimitable choice. Shall we say the Diamond Horseshoe?"

"I don't think so, thanks."

"Or The Latin Quarter?"

"Not for me, really."

"Or Leon and Eddie's? Or the Copacabana? You have only to speak the word, Phipps. Whither thou goest I will go."

Barmy said that on the whole he would prefer to attend no more cabaret performances, and Mervyn Potter accepted his decision with charming good temper.

"Then I'll tell you what we'll do. Taxi-cab driver," said Mervyn Potter, addressing the driver of a passing taxi-cab, "take us to King's Point, Long Island, and don't spare the horses. We will go and have a crack with my fiancée, Phipps."

"But, I say!"

Mervyn Potter's geniality waned. That quiet, dangerous note came into his voice.

"Have you some objection to meeting my fiancée?"

"No, no, but——"

"You have nothing against my fiancée, have you, Phipps?"

"No, no, rather not."

"So I should hope," said Mervyn Potter. "A charming girl, if ever there was one. She is a Miss Hermione Brimble, daughter of the well-known financial magnate, C. Hamilton Brimble, and by a curious coincidence of Mrs. C. Hamilton Brimble as well. You probably saw her flitting about the hotel at Skeewassett. Tallish girl with a complexion the colour of marble in starlight and eyes that glittered like emeralds when the sunlight fell on them. They are green," explained Mervyn Potter. "You'll like her enormously, and I feel sure that meeting you will set the seal on her happiness."

"But, dash it all, she won't want to see me in the middle of the night."

"You underestimate your attractiveness, Phipps. No matter what the hour, you still cast that spell of yours. If I have heard it said once, I have heard it said a hundred times, by people whose judgment I respect, that it never matters how late Cyril Fotheringay-Phipps blows in, because in the final analysis he is always Cyril Fotheringay-Phipps. Drive on, driver. When we get to King's Point, I wil direct you with word and gesture."

To reach King's Point, Long Island, one has to cross the Triborough Bridge, carry on to Great Neck and turn up the Middle Neck Road. It is a long journey and one that might have proved tedious had not Mervyn Potter enlivened it with snatches of song in a pleasant light baritone. When they arrived, it seemed to annoy him that the house should be in darkness. A stickler for etiquette, he pointed out that there ought to have been a light shining in the window to guide the wanderer home.

"A lamp. Or at least a candle. However," he said, becoming his old cheerful self again, "I suppose we must skip the red tape. That, I rather think," he went on, "is my fiancée's room and, as I see it, three courses are open to us. We can stand here and yell. Or we can throw gravel. Or you could shin up the waterpipe. Yes, that is the best plan. Up you go, Phipps. Knock twice and mention my name."

A healing thought came to Barmy.

"But your fiancée isn't there."

"How can you tell that till you've knocked?"

"You told me she was going to a dance tonight."

"So I did. Bless my soul, so I did. Well, in that case, just shin up and break the window."

'That little more,' says the poet, 'and how much it is,' If Mervyn Potter had been a shade smaller, a trifle less intoxicated, the teeniest bit less apt to take offence when thwarted, Barmy might have declined the suggestion. As it was, he felt it prudent to fall in with his companion's wishes. He was dully aware, as he started to mount the pipe, of the latter leaning against the side of the house reciting 'Excelsior' in a sonorous voice. His arrival at the sill synchronized with the verse about the maiden throwing out her kindly invitation to the young Alpine climber to stay and rest his weary head against this breast.

It was as he broke the window that from another window a little further along the house the head and shoulders of a man in a dressing-gown suddenly protruded. An electric torch shone upon Barmy, and then the man in the dressing-gown, raising a revolver, proceeded to discharge it in his direction. Bulstrode, Mrs. C. Hamilton Brimble's English butler, had heard noises in the night and, when English butlers hear noises in the night, they act.

The shots whistled harmlessly past Barmy's ears, but the hint behind them was so unmistakable that he lost no time in taking it. Mervyn Potter's startled 'Hoy!', the dog Tulip's annoyed bark and his own downward swoop were simultaneous.

When he reached the ground, Mervyn Potter had vanished into the night. But Tulip was still there. He was gargling in an offended undertone and stropping his front paws on the turf.

The mentality of dogs is odd. One might have supposed that a moment's reflection would have told Tulip that even the most unbalanced man does not climb water-pipes in order to fire revolvers at himself. Nevertheless, he was firmly convinced that it was Barmy who had been responsible for the fusillade. Looking back over the evening, it seemed to him that from start to finish Barmy had been the disrupting influence, and he was resolved to settle accounts with him once and for all. He hated horseplay. He gave his paws a final strop and advanced.

It was his quickness off the mark that saved Barmy. The merest pause for reflection, and he would have been undone. 'Oh', he said to himself, 'for the wings of a dove', and the next moment he was in the upper branches of a large cedar at the edge of the lawn. From this eminence he was able to obtain an excellent view of the subsequent proceedings.

Mervyn Potter would have had no reason now to complain of the absence of lights in the windows. The house was as brilliantly lit up as he himself. And presently figures began to emerge and search the grounds—reluctantly, it seemed to Barmy, but going through the distasteful task under the spell of the magnetism of Bulstrode, the butler, who directed the operations in his dressing-gown. Barmy had never seen a butler in a dressing-gown before, and he would willingly, impressive though it was, have forgone the experience now.

It took some little time to convince the master of the revels that a blank had been drawn, but eventually the search-party returned to the house and the lights began to go out again. The front door closed. The house was in darkness. And Barmy was just about to yield to that old familiar urge, so often felt by those who spent the evening with Mervyn Potter, to get away from it all, when the scent of a cigarette came to his nostrils and he saw that Bulstrode was standing under the tree enjoying a soothing smoke.

The sight kept him roosting on his branch, and about a quarter of an hour later there was the sound of a vehicle stopping at the gate and Mrs. C. Hamilton Brimble and her daughter Hermione came walking down the drive. He deduced that the short, stout lady was Mrs. Brimble and the taller, more slender girl her daughter from the fact that the former said 'Hermione, there is somebody under that tree', to which the latter replied 'It's Bulstrode, mother. Golly! Pipe the dressing-gown!'

It was plain that the spectacle of her butler roaming the grounds in the small hours in a dressing-gown had stirred Mrs. Brimble. Until this moment Bulstrode had been to her a suave, tail-coated figure, the keynote of whose costume was a sober grey and black. She had not known that he possessed a dressing-gown among his effects, let alone one of Chinese silk with yellow dragons embroidered on it. Her air as she advanced was that of a woman who, if her upbringing had been less careful and her social position less high, would have said 'Gee whiz!'.

"Bulstrode," she cried, "what are you doing out here at this time of night?"

The butler preserved the calm of one who knows that his story is good and worth sticking to.

"Good evening, madam, I have been pursuing burglars."

"Burglars?"

"Yes, madam. They were two in number. I heard noises and proceeded to institute an investigation, and I observed a nocturnal marauder climbing the waterpipe."

"Good gracious, Bulstrode!"

"Yes, madam."

"Who was he?"

"He did not give me his card, madam. But I recognized his accomplice, who remained at the foot of the waterpipe, reciting 'Excelsior'."

"Doing *what?*"

"Reciting 'Excelsior', madam, a poem by the late Henry Wadsworth Longfellow. Possibly the work is familiar to you? The shades of night were falling fast, madam, as through an Alpine village passed a youth who bore 'mid snow and ice, madam, a banner with——"

Mrs. Brimble stopped him. It was not that she was not fond of poetry or thought that the butler did not render it well, but she wished to stick to the agenda.

"You say you recognized him?"

"Yes, madam. It was the individual describing himself as Mervyn Potter."

"Mervyn Potter? But he dined here last night."

"Casing the joint, no doubt, madam."

The girl Hermione uttered a passionate cry.

"Bulstrode, you're cuckoo. Mervyn is not a burglar."

"I disagree with you, miss."

"He is a very celebrated motion picture star."

"That is possibly his story, miss. I can only asseverate that I caught him in the act of encouraging a young man of obviously criminal aspect to climb the waterpipe and effect an entry through a window, miss."

Mrs. Brimble intervened. Possibly, she felt that feelings were running high and that in another moment she would have an ugly brawl on her hands. If she had been a policeman, she would have said 'Break it up there, break it up'. As it was, she told Bulstrode to go to bed, and the butler with a courteous good night withdrew.

From the sound, like the expiring hiss of a syphon of soda water, which broke the silence after he had disappeared, Barmy divined correctly that his hostess had expelled a deep breath.

"So!" she said, and the ear could detect a certain generous warmth in her voice. "So this is your Mervyn! I told you, the moment I laid eyes on him——"

"I'm sure he must have some explanation, mother."

"Then let him give it," said Mrs. Brimble, and with a wave of her hand indicated a lissom figure which was emerging from the shadows across the lawn.

"Mervyn!" cried Hermione Brimble.

Mervyn Potter seemd glad to see her. There was a lover's genuine enthusiasm in his voice as he bellowed 'Hello there, babe!'.

"What are you doing here?" demanded Miss Brimble.

"Just sauntering around. As a matter of fact, I'm looking for a chap named Phipps, whom I appear to have mislaid somewhere. You may possibly know him as Fotheringay. He sometimes goes under that alias. We were thrown out of the Piazza together an hour or so ago, and while we were relaxing in the gutter, he said to me 'Potter, I would dearly love to meet your fiancée'. To which I replied 'Nothing simpler, my dear Phipps. We will hire this passing taxi-cab and tool out and see her now'."

"Mervyn, you're blotto!"

A bitter hiccough escaped Mervyn Potter.

"And who wouldn't be after an evening with Fotheringay-Phipps?" he demanded. "There's a wild Indian for you. He turned up at my apartment and intimidated me from the start. He's one of those fellows who get very ugly when sozzled, and I could see from his manner as he muscled in that he was fried to the gills. He had a gun with him. He's been blazing away with it all the evening. Slain his thousands, if you ask me. I was all in favour of a quiet home evening, a modest dinner and a couple of good books afterwards, but he would have none of it. 'I'm a timber wolf from the great frozen north-west,' he said, 'and tonight's my night to howl', and he takes me off to the Piazza. What could I do? I was helpless. He had that gun. And when we get to the Piazza and take our seats, he jumps up and shouts, 'Watch out, everybody! I'm going to start. I'm going to begin. Pick up your dead, chaps, pick up your dead. A souvenir goes with every corpse.' So they threw us out, and we landed on our ears on the sidewalk. You may take it from me that Fotheringay-Phipps is the sort of man who could get self and friend thrown out of a saloon on the Marseilles waterfront. I shall see him very sparingly after the honeymoon, I can tell you."

"There may not be a honeymoon," said Hermione Brimble grimly. "Mother, will you go in. I wish to speak to Mervyn."

She led her betrothed across the lawn, and Barmy was alone in the silent night. Relieved of the society of Mrs. C. Hamilton Brimble and her daughter Hermione, he could have descended from his perch, had he wished, but he did not wish. He could not bring himself to face whatever further shocks this house of terror might be saving up for him, and he was still clinging to his bough like a preoccupied opossum when he observed a little group returning. It consisted of Mervyn Potter, looking subdued, the dog Tulip, attached to Mervyn Potter by a leash, and Hermione Brimble, who was walking with her chin in the air. She entered the house coldly and proudly, and the front door closed behind her. No lovers' kisses had been exchanged.

Barmy climbed down—cautiously, for in a place like this you never knew what horrors might not be lurking in the shadows. The dog Tulip's passionate bound in his direction, mercifully brought up short by the leash, apprised Mervyn Potter of his presence.

"Ah, Phipps," he said dully. "I've been looking for you everywhere. Where did you spring from?"

"I was up that tree."

"You are fond of climbing trees?"

"No, I'm not fond of climbing trees. That bally man-eating dog of yours was chivvying me."

"Just playing, no doubt."

"Was he? I didn't stop to ask. I simply made the leap for life." Mervyn Potter reflected.

"You were up that tree, you say? Then you may have caught snatches of the recent conversation?"

"I did."

"But you missed the best, for by that time you were out of earshot. You aren't married, are you, Phipps?"

"No."

"Then you are probably unaware of the lengths to which an angry woman can go when putting her loved one where he belongs. I can remember nothing like it since the day when I stole a scene from a female star who was a native of Mexico. Where girls get these expressions from, I can't think. I suppose they learn them at their finishing schools."

"Has she given you the raspberry?"

"If by that you mean is the engagement off, the answer is no. We are still affianced. But at what a cost! At what a cost, Phipps! The boss has issued an ultimatum. From now on spirituous liquor is not to pass my lips. One move on my part toward the sauce, and those wedding bells will not ring out. Dating from tonight, I am on the wagon."

Mervyn Potter fell into a sombre silence, his thoughts on the grey future.

"I wonder, Phipps," he said, "if you have the slightest conception what it means to be on the wagon. I shall go through the world a haunted man. There will be joy and mirth in that world, but not in the heart of Mervyn Potter. Everywhere around me I shall hear the happy laughter of children as they dig into their Scotch highballs, but I shall not be able to join them. I shall feel like a thirsty leper. Still, if it must be, it must be. Come, east, west, home's best. Let us be getting back to New York."

"Stopping on the way for a sandwich or something?"

Mervyn Potter raised his eyebrows.

"It's incredible. Don't you ever stop eating, Phipps? Digging your grave with your teeth, that's what you are doing. Oh, well, tapeworms will be tapeworms," said Mervyn Potter philosophically.

He led the way to where the taxi-cab awaited them.

7

THE headquarters of Lehmac Productions, Inc., were situated in one of those grimy buildings that sprinkle Broadway in the Forties, the kind of building whose lifts are invariably a trifle too small and are filled with blonde girls who look exactly alike and dark-chinned men similarly cut to a pattern. One and all are in show business, or on the fringe of it, and as the lifts go up and down you hear snatches of conversation about Summer stock and camera angles and being sent for by Lindsay and Crouse.

They are mainly given up, these buildings, to the offices of those interested in Vaudeville, the films and Television. Joe Lehman had been a prominent Vaudeville agent, and it was a mark of his Vaudeville training that on becoming a producer in what is known as the legitimate he had pitched his tent in one of them. Established legitimate producers are generally to be found on top of somebody's theatre, or else hidden away in decayed brownstone fronts in Fifty-Fifth Street.

The premises of Lehmac Productions consisted of an outer hall where a pimpled office boy sat throughout the day chewing gum, a cubbyhole affording just room for a secretary and a typewriter, and an inner sanctum where Mr. Lehman held conferences with his partner, Jack McClure.

At two-thirty on the afternoon following Barmy's visit to King's Point, Long Island, he was conferring there not with Jack McClure, who was up at the Morris Rooms watching a rehearsal, but with his wife, Fanny Lehman, formerly Fanita, the World's Greatest Juggler.

It was a dingy and dishevelled apartment, very different from the rich interiors in which men like the Messrs. Lee Shubert and John Golden conduct their affairs. A sensitive decorator, suddenly introduced into it, would have winced and cried aloud. Joe Lehman's Vaudeville days lay in the quite recent past, and a pile of miscellaneous junk from his old office occupied a large part of one of the walls. There were great bundles of newspapers, most of them copies of the Christmas issue of *Variety*, containing Mr. Lehman's advertised seasonal greetings to all artists everywhere. There were a few mouldy box files, part of a stray, bespangled costume, and even a ballet dancer's slipper. Except for a huge and obviously new desk, slightly filmed with dust, the pile was the most prominent object in the room.

The rest of the furniture was also new—a swivel chair at the desk, a visitor's chair in front of it and a smaller one at one side. A water-cooler completed the list of goods and chattels, but Mr. Lehman, moving into his new quarters, had brought with him some sixty or seventy photographs of artists who at various times had availed themselves of his professional services. These decorated the walls in interesting disarray. They were all inscribed 'With love to Joe', 'To Joe from La Belle Marguery', 'To the Greatest Agent in the World' and so on—inscriptions bespeaking a business affiliation rather than a personal bond.

Mr. Lehman was seated in the swivel chair, his feet on the desk, between his lips the stump of a cigar which he chewed rhythmically. His wife, a woman in the late thirties with an enormous poise and an easy assurance acquired by years of touring the South Bends and Wichitas, preferred to pace the floor.

"Well, sir," she was saying, "I just been taking a peep at that trick troupe of yours."

"Yah?" said Mr. Lehman guardedly.

"Yessir, I seen a rehearsal, and I know now what they mean when they talk about the fate that is worse than death."

"Is that so?" said Mr. Lehman with a snarl. "Well, you keep out of them rehearsals, you hear me?"

Mr. Lehman was a large, bulky, forceful man, inclined to breathe hard in moments of professional strain. Except for a coloured shirt, his clothes were not actually loud, and yet he had the knack of making them seem so. He wore a derby hat. He always wore it. It was part of him. The most imaginative could hardly picture him bareheaded.

Fanny was not the woman to be intimidated by snarls. She continued equably.

"Yessir, you got a show there that's going to make history, do you know it? They're going to date things from the time you open this one."

Mr. Lehman stirred uneasily in the swivel chair. His hand,

moving up to scratch his head, encountered the derby hat, and he seemed to draw strength from it.

"So what's it got to do with you?" he demanded warmly. "It ain't your money, is it?"

"It would have been, if I'd of been sap enough to let you talk me into it. But I wasn't."

"All right, you wasn't. And when you wouldn't see your duty as a wife, I stepped straight down the street to Lester Burdett, and he come in for twenty grand. Quick. Just like that. He's giving me his cheque today."

"Sooner him than me," said Fanny. "I like to keep my dough."

Joe Lehman regarded her sourly. Fanny's dough was a sore subject. There ought to be some law against a wife's having a lot of money in her own name, he felt, echoing the sentiments of a thousand Broadway husbands.

"You'd have thought that after all I done for you, you'd of had some gratitude," he said morosely. "You wouldn't have had a sou if I hadn't dug you out of that Texas honky-tonk you were messing around in and put you in regular vaudeville. Fanita, the World's Greatest Juggler!" said Mr. Lehman with a wealth of satire. "If it wasn't for me, you'd be keeping four clubs in the air right now for some ten-for-a-nickel management nobody ever heard of."

Fanny bridled. Her professional pride had been touched.

"Don't you go four-clubbing me. I done six clubs for the wow at the finish, and done it for years."

"Yeah, and there ain't a stage between here and California ain't got dents in it from them clubs of yours. They wouldn't let nobody sit in the first five rows. Fanita!"

"Yes, Fanita. And I'm as good today as I ever was."

"Just about," said Mr. Lehman.

Fanny waved a nonchalant hand.

"All right, all right. I was a rotten juggler and you were a great agent. But I'm the one that's got the house and lot in Freeport, not to mention a hunk in the bank that come due this morning on a bond or sump'n. Listen, Joey," said Fanny, softening as she always did after getting a domestic quarrel out of her system. "This ain't your game. Why don't you go back to agenting, where you know the ropes?"

"Because I don't want to, see?"

Fanny sighed. A casual observer might have thought it could

not have been done, but she loved this man—fat head, cigar, derby hat and all.

"Okay," she said resignedly. "Have it your own way. Go on and produce the show and let's watch it make history, like I said."

"It'll make history all right, though not the way you mean. How can it help being a smash with Mervyn Potter starring? Every woman in America is going to come and see him."

"Unless he burns down the theatre on the opening night, and I wouldn't put it past him. If I was a producer, I'd rather manage a wagon-load of monkeys than that crazy lunatic. And personally I doubt if the customers will pay to see even Mervyn Potter, once it gets around what sort of a leading woman you've got."

"Whittaker's going to be fine."

"Is that her name? Who is she, if any?"

"She's Jack McClure's——"

"Mother?"

"Sister-in-law. She's his wife's sister. So kindly don't go getting off any of your cracks about her in front of Jack."

Fanny nodded sagely.

"So that's why she's in the show."

"No, it ain't. She's all right."

"If you like stout Dames of the Colonial Revolution. I caught that bit at the rehearsal where she's climbing up apple trees in the ancestral orchard. The stuff to make them trees out of is reinforced concrete," said Fanny, and feeling it doubtful whether she could improve on this as a last word, bestowed a kindly smile on her husband and left the room.

A few minutes later there entered a girl at the sight of whom Barmy, had he been present, would have tottered on his base and experienced a difficulty in keeping his eyes in the parent sockets. She had fair hair, and was wearing a hat that looked like a fruit salad. Her blue eyes, as they rested on Mr. Lehman, twinkled with suppressed amusement. Eileen ('Dinty') Moore, Mr. Lehman's secretary, found her employer a constant source of entertainment.

Mr. Lehman, whirling round in the swivel chair, eyed her belligerently. There was nothing in his manner to indicate that he found in her any trace of that girlish appeal which had so impressed itself on Barmy yesterday afternoon in Madison Avenue. He was still sore from the recent encounter, and to him the lodestar of Barmy's life was merely a handy underling on whom he could work off some of his pent-up feelings.

"Hey, you!"

"Yes, Admiral?"

"Where you been?"

"Lunch, Admiral."

"You've taken your time about it. And don't call me Admiral. Think I pay you to sit and stuff all day?"

"You don't pay me at all. You owe me two weeks' salary. And listen," said Dinty, feeling that this sort of thing must be checked at the outset. "The contract calls for an hour for the midday repast, and an hour's what I've had, no more, no less. So lay off, Simon Legree, and drop that cowhide whip. Don't you know that Lincoln had freed us slaves? Don't you ever read the papers?"

Mr. Lehman grunted. With Fanita, the World's Greatest Juggler, he might sometimes hope to hold his own, but when attempting to bandy words with this girl he was always uneasily conscious of an inferiority complex. If it wasn't that he owed her that two weeks' salary, thought Mr. Lehman moodily, he would have shot her out on her ear days ago, for she was as fresh, in his opinion, as a certified farm egg.

"All right," he said, conceding defeat. "Take a letter."

Dinty took several letters, for her employer loved dictating them. Presently there was a lull and, as always when these occurred, Dinty became chatty. She was a friendly little soul and liked to make the party go. She sought for a topic that would interest, elevate and amuse. She toyed for a moment with the idea of bringing up the subject of her new hat and explaining how she had got it, but decided—rightly—that this would not grip.

"I saw Mrs. Lehman at the rehearsal this morning," she said, feeling that this was more along the lines required.

"Yah?"

"She's very funny, isn't she?"

"One long scream," said Mr. Lehman, heavily.

"What's the name of the leading woman, the one who plays the heroine?"

"Gladys Whittaker."

"Gladys Whittaker," said Dinty meditatively. "And what a temper *she's* got. Why, Mrs. Lehman wasn't even talking to her."

A horrid thought writhed into Mr. Lehman's mind like a snake.

"You mean Fanny let fly with one of them wisecracks at that rehearsal?" he quavered.

"She only asked a question."

"What was it? What Whittaker's weight was? When she was born?"

"Oh, no. Though she does look kind of stout and elderly for the part, don't you think?"

"No, I don't."

"Mrs. Lehman does. We were watching the bit where Miss Whittaker is climbing up the apple tree, and Mrs. Lehman said to the director 'What does she wear in that scene?'. And the Director said 'Blue knickerbockers'."

Mr. Lehman moaned softly.

"Now it comes! The finger!"

" 'She wears blue knickerbockers,' the director said. And Mrs. Lehman said 'Drop your curtain on that laugh'."

"Miss Whittaker to see you, sir," said the pimpled office boy, appearing in the doorway.

"Wheel her in," said Dinty.

Mr. Lehman turned on her with the uninhibited warmth of some creature of the wild that has got its foot caught in a trap.

"You get out of here," he thundered, "and take them small-time jokes with you. It's bad enough I have to listen to them from Mrs. Lehman without having you start." He turned to the office boy. "Is she behaving all right?"

"Why, yes, sir."

"Not crying or nothing?"

"No, sir."

"Has she got a knife?" asked Dinty.

Mr. Lehman repeated his imitation of the trapped creature of the wild.

"Will you get out! Go type those letters."

"Yes, Massa Legree, sir."

"Bring her in," said Mr. Lehman. He spun round on Dinty once more. "What you waiting for?"

"I just want to time her to the desk," said Dinty.

If Mr. Lehman had a suitable reply to this remark, he was forced to repress it, for at this moment the office boy ushered in Miss Whittaker. Dinty, having reached the door of the cubby-hole, paused and turned.

"Yessir, blue knickerbockers," she said softly.

She went into the cubbyhole, closing the door behind her, and a moment later there came faintly through it the tapping of a typewriter.

"Well!" said Miss Whittaker.

"Don't pay no attention to her," urged Mr. Lehman. "She's loco. And don't pay no attention to Mrs. Lehman. She's loco, too. Sit down. What's on your mind?"

Miss Whittaker sat down. She was a large, spreading blonde, still handsome though a little too Junoesque to be climbing apple trees. Looking at her, one appreciated the significance of Mrs. Lehman's advice about the reinforced concrete. She carried in her hand an oblong slip of paper. This she exhibited to Mr. Lehman in the manner of a conjurer producing a rabbit from a hat.

"This is that hundred-dollar cheque of yours, Mr. Lehman. It just came back to me for the third time. What does that entitle me to? Permanent possession?"

Mr. Lehman had been through this sort of thing before.

"Wait a while and put it through again," he advised.

"I want the money, Mr. Lehman."

"You'll get it."

"May I say just one word?"

"Go ahead."

"When?" asked Miss Whittaker, limiting herself to the one word she had asked to be allowed.

Mr. Lehman's studied self-control deserted him.

"When I'm good and ready, that's when. Gosh, it's tough," cried Mr. Lehman. "Here I am, working day and night to get the show in shape, and if I get away for a minute and try to relax, in comes people asking for money. Money, money, money. If you want money, why don't you ask Jack McClure for it? You're his wife's sister."

"Jack McClure!" said Gladys Whittaker, and it was plain that she held no high opinion of her brother-in-law.

There came belatedly to Joe Lehman the thought that it might be wiser to be more conciliatory. He got up and put an affectionate arm about Miss Whittaker's shoulder. He was still wearing his hat.

"Now listen, baby," he said. "You know how it is when you're readying a show. The money's all there, but it's locked up, sort of. Frozen assets, they call it. I'll see that you get that hundred. I'm expecting a rich millionaire in any moment with a big cheque he's bringing. Gimme half an hour."

"Very well," said Miss Whittaker, with the manner of a judge pronouncing a suspended sentence. "But if that money isn't laid on the barrelhead then, I'm going straight to Equity and tell them the whole story. And you know what'll happen then. They'll call out the company."

She rose majestically and strode from the room, and Mr. Lehman, chewing his cigar, stared bleakly before him. He was thinking about Women.

Women! What a sex, what a *sex*! They came badgering you for money and talking about going straight to Equity. They bit the hand which rescued them from Texas honky-tonks. They were flip and disrespectful and looked at you oddly out of the corner of their eyes when you were dictating letters to them. He could see no percentage in the gentler sex. The man who lays a hand upon a woman, save in the way of kindness, is rightly looked askance at and viewed with concern, but Mr. Lehman could have named three on whom he would have been delighted to lay the heaviest of hands.

Presently, wincing away from this unpleasant theme, he turned to a more agreeable one. He began to muse on Lester Burdett, and immediately the dark cloud lifted. Sunshine poured into his soul. He ceased to take the dim view which he had been taking of the world because there were women in it. There might be women in the world, far too many of them, but against this you had to set the fact that the good old world also contained men like Lester Burdett, the man who had come in for twenty grand, quick, just like that.

He was still thinking loving thoughts of Lester Burdett, becoming more and more soothed the longer his mind dwelt on that square-shooting garment manufacturer, when there was a confused noise without. The door burst open, and his partner Jack McClure came tottering in, looking like something left over from the Last Days of Pompeii.

"Joe," said Jack McClure, too agitated to attempt to break the dreadful news gently. "You know what's happened? Lester Burdett has walked out on us."

★ 8 ★

JACK MCCLURE was the quiet, gentlemanly half of Lehmac Productions. It seems to be a natural law that there shall always be one quiet and gentlemanly partner in every theatrical enterprise. He was a more ingratiating type than Joe Lehman. He was even rather attractive, being tall and well built and with something of the look of the athlete about him. Joe Lehman was a man of the great indoors and at the conclusion of the business day turned his thoughts to drinks at the Astor bar. Jack McClure went off to the New York Athletic Club and played squash, and in the summer months you would find him down at Long Beach or Far Rockaway, cleaving the waves. His attire was up to the minute and a shade beyond it. He wore a fashionable grey soft hat, which, like Mr. Lehman's, never left his head.

"Walked out on us," he repeated, and going to the water-cooler helped himself to a restorative draught from a paper cup.

Mr. Lehman, who on Gladys Whittaker's departure had put his feet in their favourite position on the desk, removed them with a jerk which nearly upset the swivel chair. His face had paled. His eyes were staring. He might have been Macbeth watching the ghost of Banquo dropping in to take pot luck.

"What do you mean?"

"Just what I say. He's taking his money out of the show. Every cent."

"But why?"

"He'll tell you," said Jack McClure, pointing the paper cup at the door, through which Mervyn Potter, who had stopped to give the office boy his autograph, was now entering.

Mervyn Potter was his customary calm, affable, unruffled self. Last night's hectic doings, which might have taken the bloom off any ordinary man, had left no trace on him. His eyes were bright, his demeanour tranquil. He did not appear to have even a suspicion of a headache.

"Hail to thee, blithe Lehman," he said genially. "Quite a time

60

since we met, but you look about the same . . . unfortunately.
So does the dear old office. You seem to have put in a peck or
so more dust since I was last here, but otherwise conditions
appear to be unaltered. This is good dust," said Mervyn Potter,
running a finger over the desk. "Where do you get it?"

Mr. Lehman counted ten, for, oddly enough, his doctor had
advised the same precaution as had Mr. Anderson's.

"Never mind about my dust," he said, when the ritual was
complete. "What's all this about Lester Burdett?"

Mervyn Potter shook his head regretfully.

"A hasty man, that Burdett. One who against the advice of
the poet lets his angry passions rise. Be slow to wrath, they always
taught me at my Sunday School, but apparently no one ever sold
that idea to Lester Burdett. I don't think I have ever seen a
garment manufacturer a deeper shade of mauve. And all on
account of the merest trifle."

"Trifle?"

"He gave Lester a hot foot," said Jack McClure.

Mr. Lehman raised his hands in agony, and would have
clutched his head but for the fact that his hat was in the
way.

"A hot foot?"

"And why not? Do be reasonable, my dear Lehman," said
Mervyn Potter. "From the way you are carrying on, one would
suppose that I had been guilty of some tort or malfeasance.
I merely did what any other sensitive artist would have done in
my place. There was this Burdett asleep in his chair, and I felt—
rightly, as I think—that it was an opportunity which might not
occur again. The birds, the bees, the breeze, the trees, all Nature
in respose seemed to call to me to give him a hot foot, so I made
the gesture."

"Lester was sore," said Jack McClure, unnecessarily.

"Very," assented Mervyn Potter. "I tried to reason with him,
strove to get him to see my point of view, but he refused to listen.
The man struck me as having deaf adder blood in him. I don't
know how well you are up on deaf adders," said Mervyn Potter,
"but their leading characteristic is a disinclination to hearken to
the voice of charmers, charming never so wisely."

Mr. Lehman was a man easily stirred and prompt, when stirred,
to express his emotion in burning words. He called Mervyn
Potter six derogatory names in rapid succession, and Mervyn

Potter said genially that he betted Mr. Lehman said that to all
the girls.

"Smile on me, Lehman," said Mervyn Potter. "A forced,
bitter smile, if you will, but only smile. Good heavens, I can't
see what all the fuss is about. Why, in Hollywood giving a hot
foot is just one of the common courtesies of everyday life."

"To hell with Hollywood!"

"An admirable sentiment," said Mervyn Potter, "and one
which I have often voiced myself."

Mr. Lehman replaced his feet on the desk. He could think
better that way, and if ever there was a time for thinking, and
thinking clearly, this was it. Twenty thousand dollars gone, just
like that. It served him right, he felt, for ever supposing that
anyone outside the violent ward of a lunatic asylum could handle
a star like Mervyn Potter. The only bright spot in the whole
black business, the only faint suggestion of a silver lining in the
cloud that enveloped him, was that Fanita, the World's Greatest
Juggler, was not among those present to say 'I told you so'.

Jack McClure had refilled his paper cup. He sipped at it glumly.

"Well, there goes the ball game," he said.

Mr. Lehman nodded with equal despondency.

"Yah, we'll have to close the show."

"Why on earth?" said Mervyn Potter.

"Why?" snarled Mr. Lehman. "Maybe you'll tell me where
I can find another prospect to pry himself loose from twenty
grand?"

"That's what Lester was coming across with," said Jack
McClure. "Twenty thousand."

Mervyn Potter seemed amazed.

"Twenty thousand?" he said. "The merest chicken-feed. Why,
in Hollywood we provide free bread and soup kitchens for the
poor devils who are down to twenty thousand dollars. We give
them our old clothes."

Mr. Lehman shot a baleful look at him.

"Will you stop talking about what you do in Hollywood. This
is Broadway, and guys willing to put twenty grand into a show
don't grow on bushes."

"This is the pessimist in you speaking, Lehman. Correct this
defeatist attitude. Good heavens, man," said Mervyn Potter,
"for a play starring God's clean-cut, square-jawed gift to American
womanhood, you don't have to go around with a hat, saying

'Brother, can you spare a dime?' Big business men with double chins and bags under their eyes will fight for the privilege of paying their tribute to Art. Why, there was a young millionaire at Skeewassett who was pleading to be allowed to invest his all in the venture."

"What!" said Mr. Lehman, leaping.

"What!" said Jack McClure, skipping like the high hills.

"Who is he?" said Mr. Lehman.

"Where is he?" said Jack McClure.

"Ah, there you have me," said Mervyn Potter. "His name is Phipps, but where he is I could not say. I ran into him yesterday, but omitted to ascertain his address. But you'll find him, you'll find him," said Mervyn Potter. "Just hunt around." And feeling that he had done all that human power could do for these men, he picked up his hat from the desk and withdrew.

Mr. Lehman was the first to speak as the door closed.

"Gimme that telephone book," he said.

Jack McClure handed him the telephone directory, and he turned its pages feverishly.

"There's forty-one Phippses listed," he announced, having counted.

"Call 'em all," said Jack McClure.

"I don't have to call 'em all," said Mr. Lehman shrewdly. "No need to bother about Mrs. Anna B. Phipps or Phipps Astor Stationery or Edgar E. Phipps, photographer, or Mrs. Edward H. Phipps or Mrs. Elsie Phipps or Mrs. Florence Phipps or Mrs. Grenaline Phipps or the Phipps Guest Agency, Inc." He took up the telephone. "Get me Phipps," he said.

"Sir?" said the pimpled office boy.

"Gimme Phipps."

"Which Phipps, sir?"

"All the Phippses there are, except Mrs. Anna B. Phipps, Phipps Astor Stationery, Edgar E. Phipps, photographer, Mrs. Edward H. Phipps, Mrs. Elsie Phipps, Mrs. Florence Phipps, Mrs. Grenaline Phipps and the Phipps Guest Agency, Inc.

"Yessir," said the pimpled office boy, alertly dialling the number of Edgar E. Phipps, photographer.

Time passed. Presently a hoarse and exhausted Joseph Lehman leaned back in his swivel chair, mopping his forehead. He had chatted with more Phippses than probably any other man in New York. They included bass Phippses, tenor Phippses, baritone

Phippses, three Phippses with colds in the head, two Phippses who stuttered and one final supreme Phipps who appeared to have no roof to his mouth.

"Now what?" he said. A sudden inspiration came to him. He spoke into the telephone. "Gimme David."

"All the Davids, sir?" said the pimpled office boy, who was beginning to warm to his work.

"Sol David."

"Yes sir."

"Sol might come through," said Mr. Lehman.

"He might," said Jack McClure.

"This show's a pipe, and any bird that comes in is going to make plenty."

The telephone rang.

"Is Sol David there? This is Joe Lehman speaking. Oh . . . NO!" Mr. Lehman hung up the receiver. "Bermuda!" he said bitterly. "Beats hell how far away they can get when you're trying to raise coin."

Jack McClure had a suggestion.

"Here's a slant. There was two fellows named Levi, in ladies' shirt waists, sunk some dough in a show last year."

Mr. Lehman shook his head.

"They got bit. They're off the stuff for life. So here I am with a compact little drama, up to the minute, and I can't——"

Jack McClure had another suggestion.

"Can't you get it out of Fanny?"

"Fanny!"

"She's got plenty."

"Don't I know it! I was around at her bank this morning trying to find out what her balance was, but no dice. Fanny won't part. She's so tight she could carry an armful of eels up two flights of stairs and not drop one. There's that damned telephone again. You answer it, Jack. My throat's on fire."

Mr. Lehman, infringing Mr. McClure's copyright, went dully to the water-cooler and filled a paper cup.

"WHAT!!!" cried Jack McClure, at the telephone.

Mr. Lehman dropped the cup. Jack McClure placed a hand over the mouthpiece, and spoke in a trembling voice.

"Phipps!" he said.

"What Phipps? Edgar E., photographer?"

"No, no, no."

"The Phipps Guest Agency?"

"No, no, no. The right Phipps."

Mr. Lehman tottered like some forest giant beneath the axes of lumbermen.

"The *right* Phipps?"

"Says Mervyn Potter told him we might possibly let him have a slice of the show."

"Where is he?" asked Mr. Lehman tensely.

"Phoning from the Astor," said Jack McClure, having consulted the instrument. "Wait in the lobby," he proceeded, still speaking into the telephone. "I'll come and fetch you."

"Yah, do," said Mr. Lehman. "And hey!" he shouted, as his partner made for the door. "Keep hold of his arm!"

Mr. Lehman's lassitude had left him. He became a thing of fire and energy.

"Moore!" he bellowed.

Dinty appeared from the cubbyhole.

"Yes, Colonel?"

"Clean this place up. There's a big angel coming."

"Yes, sir."

"And shake a leg."

"Yes, sir. Who did you say was coming?"

"An angel. A millionaire. He's going to put money in the show."

"Three rousing cheers. Does that mean you'll pay me my salary?"

"So you're going to begin now, huh?"

"You owe me two weeks."

"All right, all right. You'll get it, you'll get it. And look here. When the guy's been here awhile, you make an entrance with a piece of paper, see? A letter—anything—make it busy—put it on my desk."

"Yes, sir."

"Don't stop to take no bows. Just exit."

"Yes, sir. This sounds like one of those new round games that sweep Society like a forest fire."

"Never you mind what it sounds like. Have you got it?"

"Yes, General."

"Come in. Bring a paper. Put it on desk——"

"And exit smiling. You couldn't tell me what that's supposed to accomplish, could you?"

"Never you mind what it's supposed to accomplish. It's

atmosphere, dammit, if you really want to know. Ain't you never heard of atmosphere?"

"Oh, atmosphere?" said Dinty. "Excuse it, please," and went back into her cubbyhole, while Mr. Lehman, putting his feet up on the desk, tilted his derby hat over his eyes, lit a fresh cigar and gave himself up to the first really pleasant thoughts he had had today. He was not deeply religious, but he could not but feel that there was something impressive in the way Providence looked after the good man and saw to it that he did not fall by the wayside. The good man might be down, but with Providence in his corner, handling the towel, he was never out.

It is possible that Mr. Lehman might have burst into song like a skylark, so uplifted was his mood, but before he could proceed to this awful extreme Jack McClure appeared in the doorway, ushering in the Last of the Fotheringay-Phippses.

He was holding Barmy's arm in an affectionate grip.

"This is Mr. Cyril Phipps, Joe," he said. "Mr. Lehman, Mr. Phipps."

★ 9 ★

THE instant Mr. Lehman's eyes rested on Barmy, he realized that he had underestimated the lengths to which Providence was prepared to go when showering its blessings on the good man. 'I seen in a minute he was our oyster,' Mr. Lehman would have said, if he had been dictating his Memoirs to a stenographer. 'Built to order,' he would have added. '*With* watercress.' There was an engaging air of innocence about the young man that stirred the senior partner of Lehmac Productions like a bugle.

"How are you, my blossom?" he said. "Take a seat."

Barmy settled himself in a gingerly manner in the visitor's chair. Mr. Lehman had made a deep impression on him. There was about this theatrical magnate something of J. G. Anderson and a suggestion of Barmy's Uncle Theodore, a man who from childhood's earliest days had always been able to turn a nephew's blood to ice with a glance. He had his hat in his hand, and noticing that Mr. Lehman and Mr. McClure were wearing theirs, thought for a moment of putting it on his head, but was not quite equal to it.

"Have a cigar?" said Mr. Lehman.

"Eh? No, I don't think I will, thanks fearfully."

"Okay," said Mr. Lehman agreeably. He cocked an eye at Barmy, drinking him in. "Where you from?"

"Well, London originally."

"London, England?"

"That's right."

"Great place. I never played it myself, but they all tell me. So you're interested in the theatre, Mr. Phipps? Ever been in show business?"

"Not yet."

"Well, we've all got to begin. The great thing is to find a great play, like I done. I got a show, my puss, that's the biggest dramatic novelty in twenty years. There ain't never been nothing like it, see?"

"No?"

"Nothing," said Mr. Lehman, and there was an impressive pause while he meditated on the bigness of his dramatic novelty.

Jack McClure broke it by coughing in his quiet, gentlemanly way.

"I was telling Mr. Phipps," he said, "that providing he acts quick, maybe he could get in on it. We haven't quite completed our financing, have we?"

"Not quite," admitted Mr. Lehman.

"Lucky," said Jack McClure.

"Very lucky," said Mr. Lehman. "Well, of course, Mr. Phipps, here in New York it's just like Mr. McClure says. You got to make quick decisions. Think on your feet. There was a friend of ours could have bought in on *Arsenic And Old Lace* if he'd of snapped it up."

"He waited till next day," said Jack McClure sadly, "and it was too late."

"That's the show game," said Mr. Lehman, shaking his head.

"That's the show game," said Jack McClure, shaking his.

Barmy nodded intelligently.

"I see what you mean. Do It Now, as it were. Well, I'm all for quick decisions myself, if it's really a red-hot proposition. Only, of course, I've got to be careful, what? Pretty cautious and wary, if you see what I mean."

"Just the kind of man I like, sweetheart. I ain't asking you to go in blindfold. I got a great gag and I ain't afraid to show it. I got a play that's going to catch everybody, see? It ain't highbrow, and yet it ain't lowbrow."

"Sort of medium brow?"

"Yah. It's the first good medium brow show they've had, and it's going to be a knock-out."

"Going to make a lot of money, what?"

"Money? I'll say! Ask Dick Rodgers and Oscar Hammerstein what they're knocking down out of this *South Pacific*. Ask Oscar Serlin what he made out of *Life With Father*. Ask Max Gordon what he cleaned up out of *Born Yesterday*."

"You want me to ask them?"

"I'll tell you, sweetheart. Millions."

"Millions?"

"Millions," said Mr. Lehman.

"Millions," said Jack McClure.

"Well, that's what I'd like," said Barmy. "Only I'd want it to be safe."

"I'll guarantee it personally. So will my friend here. Won't you, Jack?"

"Sure."

"So what do you say? Think on your feet. That's show business."

Barmy fingered his Drones Club tie. Mr. Lehman's eloquence had stirred him deeply, but he could not forget that good thing of his Uncle Theodore's which he had heard so often both as a boy and when grown to manhood. 'Look before you leap,' his Uncle Theodore had been fond of saying, for he was a neat phrase-maker.

"Could I read the play or something?" he asked.

"H'm," said Mr. Lehman doubtfully. "Think we can dig up a script for Mr. Phipps, Jack?"

"Afraid not," said Jack McClure, correctly interpreting that 'H'm'. "You see, the troupe's in rehearsal, Mr. Phipps, and they're using them all."

"And what the hell! You don't need no script," said Mr. Lehman. "I'll show you where it's sure fire." With a sweeping gesture he pushed the litter on the desk out of his way. It was as if a battleship had been cleared for action. Joe Lehman was about to begin. "Now look," he said, tilting his hat back. "It's a play about a feller with a heart of gold, see? Feller who's always trying to do the square thing by everybody."

"A gentleman in every sense of the word," said Jack McClure.

"A gentleman in every sense of the word," said Mr. Lehman. "Mervyn Potter plays the part, and will he play it to the queen's taste? Ask me."

"Will he?"

"Yes," said Mr. Lehman.

"Yes," said Jack McClure.

"You betcher," siad Mr. Lehman.

"You betcher," said Jack McClure.

"Well, that's fine," said Barmy.

Mr. Lehman tilted his hat sideways.

"Now look. We open with a Prologue."

"A Prologue," explained Jack McClure.

"There's a playwright in the Prologue."

"Fellow who writes plays," said Jack McClure.

"And he's in love with a dame, see? And he's asked a bunch of people to come around and hear him read his new drama. Including the skirt. So he starts to read, and he says 'The first scene is an orchard'. Now!" Mr. Lehman juggled briefly with his hat. "When he says 'orchard', we work that cutback trick, like in the movies. Black out, quick change, lights up, and it's the orchard."

"Just the way he said."

"Yah. Then all the rest of it is his play. Only he's in it, see, and the dame's in it, see. This doll that's in the orchard is the same doll you seen in the Prologue. Neat?"

"Frightfully neat," said Barmy.

"She's climbing up an apple tree. On account she's in high spirits," explained Mr. Lehman. "And along comes this feller that was the playwright in the Prologue, and they gab awhile back and forth, and he tells her he loves her, and she says she loves him, so there they are, all set to get married."

Barmy blinked. The story, as outlined, seemed to him to lack dramatic complications. A bit on the short side, too. Raise the curtain at eight-forty, Eastern Standard time, and it would fall, he estimated, at about eight-fifty-three.

"Is that the end of the play?" he asked.

"End of the play? Wait!" said Mr. Lehman. "You ain't heard nothin' yet."

"There's some more coming?"

"You bet there's some more coming."

"Don't forget the priest," said Jack McClure.

"Oh, yah. There's a priest comes in, see, and there's some gab with him. Well, orchard scene over, we cut to a big cabaret in New York. Music and dancing. You know."

"Yah," said Barmy, risking it.

"And into this cabaret comes the feller, the dame and the dame's brother. The feller and the dame ain't married yet. They're going to be tomorrow. Get it?"

"Yah," said Barmy, quite confidently this time.

"Now, this brother of the dame's is one of them wild young sons of guns, always cutting up and raising hell, and a feller comes along that don't like him and says 'Oh, it's you, is it?', and the brother gives him a dirty look and says 'Yah. Want to make something of it?" and the feller . . . well, one thing and another happens, both of them getting uglier every minute, and back and forth and back and forth, and so on and so on, and first thing you know the brother outs with a gun, and *bingo!*" said Mr. Lehman, climaxing the episode with an explosive snap of the fingers.

"I say!" said Barmy. "Hot stuff, what? Shoots him, does he?"

"Deader than a mackerel. Lays him out colder than a step-mother's kiss. Music stops. Waiters yell. Girls scream. Women faint. And in comes the police. 'What goes on?' asks the police," said Mr. Lehman, now giving a performance of which Edwin Booth would have been proud. " 'Who dun it?' says the police. And the feller says he dun it."

"The feller?"

"Yah."

"But he's dead."

"Who's dead?"

"The feller."

"No, no, no," said Mr. Lehman, clutching his hat. "Not that feller. The other feller. The feller that's nuts on the dame. The hero. He says 'I dun it', to save the brother of the woman he loves."

Barmy was mildly puzzled.

"But weren't there a lot of people in the vicinity?"

"Sure they was."

"Then don't they see the brother shoot the feller?"

"Naw," said Mr. Lehman, with vast scorn for the novice's ignorance of stage mechanics. "They're all looking the other way."

"Oh, I see. Right ho."

"So the feller's arrested and gets twenty years in the cooler, only you don't know that till the next act. We end at Act One with the arrest. The cops put the bracelets on the feller, and the feller goes out with his chin up and the dame lets out a screech and falls in a swoon as the curtain drops, and that's your Act One. Great start, huh?"

"Oh, terrific."

"It's called *Sacrifice*," said Jack McClure. "He sacrifices himself for the dame, see?"

" 'Sacrifice'," said Mr. Lehman. "Good marquee title, huh?"

"Eh?"

"It'll look well up in lights," said Jack McClure.

"Oh, stupendous," said Barmy.

Mr. Lehman had employed the intermission between the acts by refreshing himself at the water-cooler. He cleared himself for action again.

"Now! Second Act. It's twenty years later, and the feller's out of jail. He's gone to hide his head in one of them South Sea islands, and he's gone down and down, and now he's so far down, he's playing the piano in one of them places," said Mr. Lehman delicately.

"House of ill fame," said Jack McClure.

"Yah, house of ill fame," said Mr. Lehman. "He's a broken man playing the piano in a house of ill fame."

"Don't forget the priest," said Jack McClure.

"Oh, yah. This priest. Remember him?"

"He was in the orchard."

"That's him. He's a missionary now, working in this South Sea island, and he comes to close this place up, and you get a big scene. There's a big party going on, everybody cutting up, and he comes in and opens up on them. And suddenly, *zowie!* This feller, the hero, comes back at him. That's where we bring in the strong talk. He calls him all kinds of names. We go the limit. He says 'You missionaries is all alike, you don't give nobody no chance', and back and forth and back and forth and so-and-so and so-and-so and so-and-so, and that's the end of your first scene, Act Two."

"Lots of action," said Barmy judicially.

"Nothing to what comes later. Next scene is in the Governor's house."

"Whose governor?"

"The Governor of the island."

"Oh, ah."

"And who's come to visit the Governor in the course of one of them around-the-world cruises but the dame that was going to marry the hero and her husband, because she married this other guy while the hero was in the coop. And the hero's seen her driving to the house, and late that night he breaks in. Feels he must have a word with her, see? So it's her bedroom and she's in a negligay, and in comes the hero through the window and says 'Genevieve!', and she says 'Harold!', and she says 'Is it you?', and he says 'Yah, it's me', and back and forth and back and forth, and then it comes out that the brother has died and confessed on his death-bed that it was him that dun it, and she says she loves the hero still but must stick to this guy she's married because she's the soul of honour, see, and they have a farewell scene, and suddenly in comes the husband and he thinks the hero is a burglar and he plugs him with his gun and the hero falls to the ground a corpse and the dame falls on top of him and has a fit and dies on his body. The next act's in heaven," said Mr. Lehman, going to the water-cooler.

Barmy blinked.

"Heaven?"

"Heaven," said Mr. Lehman, emptying his paper cup. "Here's where we got all those angels coming down the aisles——"

"Long veils over them" said Jack McClure.

"Everything's all mixed up in this act. The Governor's there, only he's supposed to be God."

"Is that all right to do?"

"There was a big hit done it," said Mr. Lehman in a tone calculated to lay all doubts. "Anyhow, we don't really say it."

"Don't forget the priest," said Jack McClure.

"Oh, yah. This priest comes in and he's got a rabbi with him, see? And they talk about how everybody's the same underneath and it don't matter what religion they got. And back and forth and back and forth and so on and so on, and then suddenly *bingo*! Black out, quick change, and lights go up on the playwright's home, and the playwright's got the dame in his arms and she says the blue-bird of happiness was at home all the time. Kiss, finish reading the play, everybody says great, the feller and the dame gets married, fade out, and curtain. How do you like it?" said Mr. Lehman.

Barmy mopped his forehead.

"Terrific. Who wrote it?"

"Some guy, I forget his name. We bought him out, so of course we don't have to pay royalties. You can't lose with it, sweetheart. Now how much was you thinking of putting up? You can have forty-nine per cent for . . ." Mr. Lehman paused, measuring his man. "For thirty thousand dollars," he concluded.

"Oh, I say, dash it! Thirty thousand?"

"Can't you shave it a little, Joe, for Mr. Phipps?" asked Jack McClure, and Mr. Lehman said he thought it might be possible.

"I'll tell you what I'll do. Give me a quick yes and I'll take twenty-five."

"I'm afraid the binge is off," said Barmy.

He rose disconsolately, but not for long. Four willing hands pressed him into the chair again.

"This coin of yours," said Mr. Lehman. "If it was where you could dig it up in a hurry, maybe we can do business."

"It's in a bank on Fifth Avenue."

"It is? Well, I wasn't going to of let it go for this," said Mr. Lehman, "but you give me your cheque for ten thousand, and twenty-five per cent of the show is yours."

"You couldn't have bought in on *Harvey* for that," said Jack McClure.

"And that was a big hit, too," said Mr. Lehman, handsomely. "Now what do you say?"

Barmy fingered his tie. A man whose worldly assets consist of twenty-two thousand dollars and eighteen cents may legitimately finger his tie before deciding to invest ten thousand of it in a little drama, however compact and up to the minute.

"Ten thousand?"

"That's the dope."

"Ten thousand?"

"And it's a bargain. Think on your feet."

Barmy rose slowly.

"Well . . ."

"Set!" cried Mr. Lehman.

"Set!" cried Jack McClure.

The two partners became two live wires. With a quick movement Mr. Lehman dipped a pen in the ink and proffered it to Barmy, while simultaneously Jack McClure cleared a space on the desk. Their every gesture showed that immediate action was expected, and Barmy, with something of the emotions of a man who is going over Niagara Falls in a barrel and realizes that it is too late to turn back, slowly began to draw out his chequebook. Two pairs of eyes followed his every move. It was, indeed, with difficulty that the Messrs. Lehman and McClure restrained themselves from taking the book out of his hands and spreading it open on the table. Barmy, still slowly, opened it himself. He took the pen from Mr. Lehman's hand, and began to write.

"Guaranty Trust, eh?" said Jack McClure, peering over his shoulder.

"Joe Le-h-m-a-n," said Mr. Lehman helpfully. "You're a smart baby, Mr. Phipps, and you're going to clean up. Now just sign it."

Barmy poised the pen in the air, and, as he did so, there was a noise outside like the sudden rising of a hundred pheasants and the door was flung open explosively.

The wife of Mr. Lehman's bosom strode in.

"Listen, you dog-faced four-flusher!" she said, addressing Mr. Lehman, and slammed the door behind her with a devastating bang.

✱ 10 ✱

WITH a speed remarkable in a man so heavily built, Mr. Lehman sprang from his swivel chair and was at her side. He had no means of knowing what was the motive which had caused the moon of his delight to play this return date, but he feared the worst. The look which she was giving him presaged disaster. To say that the World's Greatest Juggler was glaring would be to convey too weak an impression. It seemed to Mr. Lehman's fevered imagination that flames were shooting from her eyes. Quaking inwardly, he sought refuge in bluster.

"Ain't you got no sense at all?" he demanded heatedly. "Get out of here. Get out of here."

For a moment the emotions with which Fanny was wrestling were too deep for words. Then she found speech.

"Listen!"

"Now, Fanny——" moaned Mr. Lehman.

"Fanny, for the love of——" cried Jack McClure.

Fanny was deaf to these appeals. She had a powerful voice, and she raised it to its utmost. The pimpled office boy, who, when the door had slammed, had feared that he was going to be left out of this, experienced a sense of relief and pressed his ear more closely to the keyhole.

"Listen!" said Fanny, all the woman in her flashing from her eyes. "I just come from my bank. And the paying teller there says there was a guy around there this morning with a check suit and a trick tie trying to find out how big my balance was."

Mr. Lehman shot an appreciative glance at Barmy.

"Now, now," he said, as soothingly as was within his power, "I don't know nothing about it. Come back after a while," he urged.

"If you show up around there again," proceeded the voice of doom, "they got instructions to shoot on sight. They'll wait till they see the whites of your eyes, then *bong*. That's all I come to tell you."

"Then get out!"

"I'm not staying. I'm only telling you not to go snooping around my money, because you ain't going to get a nickel of it," said Fanny. She flung open the door, and the office boy retreated, rubbing his ear. "No, sir, not a nickel," concluded Fanny. "Not for a rotten show like that."

She went out, and the door crashed shut behind her.

For an appreciable space of time after her departure neither Mr. Lehman nor Jack McClure moved. Only their eyes travelled round to Barmy, who was sitting rigidly in the visitor's chair. Then Mr. Lehman began to slide back to his place at the desk— slowly, casually, pitifully trying to give the impression that nothing had happened. Jack McClure likewise shifted his position, but neither man allowed his eyes to stray for an instant from Barmy. If Barmy had been the statue of the Winged Victory in the Louvre and they two art-loving tourists, they could not have regarded him with a more single-minded intentness.

Barmy came to life. He raised the pen, then suddenly lowered it and looked up.

"Did she say rotten?" he asked in a low voice.

Mr. Lehman was himself again.

"She wasn't talking about this show," he said quickly.

"It's another one we got," said Jack McClure.

"She don't even know nothing about this one," said Mr. Lehman.

"Who was it? A friend of yours?"

"It was my old lady. Mrs. Lehman. She's loco. Pay no attention to her. She has these spells."

There was a pause. Barmy's face, both men were distressed to observe, was still sicklied o'er with the pale cast of thought. Mr. Lehman addressed him pleadingly.

"Now listen, blossom boy, you got judgment of your own, ain't you? A smart guy like you. I told you about the show. Don't it sound like a wow?"

"Oh, definitely. But . . . on the other hand. You see, I'm not so dashed keen on losing ten thousand dollars."

Mr. Lehman achieved an amused chuckle.

"You ain't going to lose it. Did I tell you about the bookings?"

"Bookings?"

"The towns we play in. The theatres." Mr. Lehman reached into the drawer for the route sheet. "Look. We open in Syracuse, see? A great show town. Then we go to Providence, Worcester, Albany . . . all them soft spots."

"They're soft, are they?"

"They're great. We got the cream. So just sign that cheque and we'll be set."

Barmy continued to hesitate. Two voices were ringing in his ears—one the voice of Fanita, the World's Greatest juggler, the other that of his Uncle Theodore. When he closed his eyes, as he now did, he seemed to see his Uncle Theodore standing warming his ample trousers-seat at the fire in the library at home, fixing him with a fishy gaze and coming through with that look-before-you-leap sequence which was so often on his lips. Useless to attempt to conceal from himself that Uncle Theodore would take a very pale view of what was going on in the office of Lehmac Productions, Inc.

It was as he sat there with closed eyes, wondering what to do for the best, that he heard the click of a door handle. Light footsteps sounded on the office linoleum. He opened his eyes and sat staring, spellbound by what he saw.

A girl of about the tonnage of Betty Grable was leaning over Mr. Lehman's desk, laying on it what looked like a letter, and a single glance enabled him to recognize her as the girl who since that romantic meeting in Madison Avenue had never left his thoughts for a moment, except possibly the moment when he was soaring into the boughs of the cedar a short head in front of the dog Tulip. He uttered a wordless cry, and Dinty, looking up, recognized him in her turn. She did not speak, for discipline is discipline, but her eyes widened and she gave him one of her friendliest smiles. Then she went back to her cubbyhole, and Barmy gaped after her, transfixed.

"I say," he said dazedly.

Mr. Lehman was studying the letter frowningly.

"From the Theatre Guild," he said to Jack McClure. "They want to buy in on the show."

"I thought they would."

"Yah."

"You were sort of expecting to hear from them after what they were saying Tuesday."

"Yah. Of course it's too late now. We've promised Mr. Phipps."

"We can't let Mr. Phipps down."

"No, we got to do the square thing by Mr. Phipps. It's the same old story. They didn't think on their feet, so they lost out. That's show business," sighed Mr. Lehman.

"That's show business," sighed Jack McClure.

Barmy was not interested in the misfortunes of the Theatre Guild. He was still gaping at the door of the cubbyhole.

"I say," he said. "Who was that?"

"Huh?"

"That girl."

"Oh, her? My secretary."

"Your secretary?"

"Yah."

Barmy quivered from head to foot. Soft music seemed to him to be playing in the office of Lehmac Productions and violets to be sprouting from its dusty floor.

"You mean she works here?"

"Sure. All the time."

Barmy ceased to hesitate. Faintly, as from a great distance, he could still hear Uncle Theodore's warning voice, but he had no leisure to listen to Uncle Theodore now. With a firm hand he signed the cheque, and Mr. Lehman jumped at it like a trout leaping at a fly.

"It's wet," said Barmy.

"I'll dry it. Well, my puss," said Mr. Lehman, "you're a partner now." He sprang for the door, where Jack McClure was already standing like a greyhound straining at the leash. "You wait here, see, while Jack and me go to the bank. You wait here and look after things. I'll tell you what. Hey!" he bellowed.

Dinty appeared.

"Look out for this gentleman till we get back," said Mr. Lehman. "Come on, Jack."

The door closed behind them.

Dinty was the first to break the silence which followed the exodus of the two partners, for Barmy, confronted at this close range with a girl who would have affected him like a blow from a blunt instrument even if seen through a telescope, was having trouble with his vocal cords. Electric shocks were passing through him, and his toes curled inside their suède shoes.

"So we meet again," said Dinty. "Properly introduced this time. Though it wasn't much of an introduction, was it?"

Barmy was now able to articulate.

"Eh?" he said, speaking almost fluently.

"He might at least have mentioned our names."

"Names? You want to know my name?"

"Well, it would be convenient to have it, so that I could tell whether to address you as Judge or Colonel or Your Royal Highness. Mine, by the way, is Dinty Moore."

"Dinty?"

"All Moores are called Dinty. Because of the restaurant."

"What restaurant?"

"Dinty Moore's. Don't you know Dinty Moore's? It's like Lindy's."

"What's Lindy's?"

Dinty saw that this was going to take some time.

"Suppose we just let it go, shall we?" she suggested. "What's your name?"

"Mine?" Barmy thought for a moment. "Oh, Fotheringay—I mean Phipps."

"Well, which?"

"Eh?"

"Is it Fotheringay or Phipps?"

"It's both."

Dinty frowned, as if at some smooth sophistry which in her opinion could only cloud the issue.

"It can't be both."

"There's a hyphen in the middle."

"That may be your story, but it sounds thin to me."

"As a matter of fact, it isn't exactly Fotheringay, if you follow me."

"I don't."

"It's pronounced Fungy."

"You can't pronounce Phipps Fungy."

"No, the Fotheringay."

"You said it wasn't Fotheringay."

"No, it isn't."

Dinty's sternness seemed to deepen. It was plain that she was beginning to feel that she was being played fast and loose with.

"I don't like this shiftiness and evasion," she said. "What do you expect to gain by it? Be frank. Be open. Let your Yea be Yea and your Nay Nay, your Phipps Phipps and your Fungy Fungy."

"My pals all call me Barmy."

"Now we're getting somewhere."

"I wish you would call me Barmy."

"I'd love to. Thank you, Barmy."

"Not at all."

There was a pause.

"Well," said Dinty, "and how's the arson business?"

"Eh?"

"Been setting any more hats on fire?"

"Oh, no, rather not."

"Bungalows?"

"Oh, no. No bungalows."

"Turned over a new leaf, have you, and decided to go straight? I was hoping you would. It's just a matter of will power. And what have you been doing since we last met?"

"Me? Oh, nothing much. I was chased up a tree by a dog last night."

"You do live, don't you? I went to a party up in the Bronx last night, and you'll be glad to hear the new hat was a sensation. I was chased up a staircase by a Television master of ceremonies."

There was another pause. Barmy sought in his tottering mind for topics that would keep the conversation going. He was aware that his contribution to it so far had not been of an outstanding brilliance, and wished to remedy this as soon as possible. He also wished that the top of his head would stop going up and down like the lid of a kettle, for this interfered with clear thought.

"Lots of dust in here," he said, hitting on something bright.

"Yes, we're proud of our dust," said Dinty. "Mr. Lehman has it imported specially. Some of it's got on your face. No, not there. More to the left. Here, let me do it."

She took the handkerchief from his hand and removed the alluvial deposit.

It was a process which involved a close proximity between them, and it was a dangerous moment for a girl who had made so profound an impression on a Fotheringay-Phipps to come into close proximity with him, for the blood of the Fotheringay-Phippses is notoriously hot. It was Barmy's Uncle Theodore—this can be verified by consulting the family archives—whose hot blood got him into all that trouble with the barmaid at Oxford in the year 1909.

Barmy, moreover, influenced by the remarks of the Gypsy Sybil, had come to look upon this girl as his destined mate, and it is pretty generally recognized by poets of the romantic school that when you meet your destined mate, formalities can be dispensed with and the etiquette book disregarded. A brief 'Hullo, there' and you are at liberty to express yourself.

This may be right, or it may be wrong—poets are uncertain guides—but, wrong or right, it was the view which Barmy took. Whatever it was that was lifting the top of his head suddenly boiled over. Sparks danced before his eyes. He reached out impulsively, folded Dinty in a warm embrace, and kissed her.

He kissed her with all the pent-up passion of a generous nature, and was about to continue along these lines when a hand, whizzing up, smote him on the left ear. Heaven, as is well known, protects the working girl, but Dinty Moore on occasions like this always found it more convenient not to rely solely on help from above. She packed a nice uppercut in both hands and was not afraid to use it. In just such a manner she had smitten a young insurance clerk named Ed one evening at Coney Island when, on the strength of having bought her two hot dogs and a chocolate nut sundae, he had behaved in a similarly impulsive manner.

She stepped back and regarded Barmy coldly. He had disappointed her. She was feeling as she would have felt if she had stopped to fraternize with a dog of amiable aspect, and the dog had turned and bitten her.

Barmy rubbed his ear. He was still not thinking clearly, but he could see that an apology was in order.

"I'm sorry," he said.

"Don't mention it."

"I lost my head."

"If you call it a head. Did I hurt you?"

"Yes."

"Good," said Dinty.

Barmy's mind began to work again. He was able to explain.

"It was a bit sudden, I know. I got carried away. You see, a fortune-teller over in England told me I should take a long journey and meet a fair girl, so when I took the long journey and met you, I naturally said to myself 'What ho!'. I mean, I saw in a second that there you were and there I was. There we both were, if you follow me. I oughtn't to have let myself be carried away like that, but I was sort of leading up to ask you if you'd marry me."

"What!"

"Marry. M. for measles."

Dinty seated herself on the desk, and eyed him with a bright interest. Hers had been a sheltered life, and this was the first time she had encountered anything like the Last of the Fotheringay-Phippses.

"Well!" she said.

"I know, I know. Of course, you'll want to think it over. I hadn't meant to spring it on you quite so soon."

"It sort of slipped out?"

"That's right. I fell in love with you at first sight, don't you know, and all that sort of rot, but I had rather intended to hush it up till a more suitable moment."

"Have you often fallen in love at first sight?"

"Never with the same——"

"Fervour?"

"That's right. Fervour."

"F for fried potatoes?"

"Exactly."

Dinty continued to gaze at him, fascinated. She was still doing so, when the door opened and Miss Gladys Whittaker came in, walking grimly and purposefully. Expecting to see Mr. Lehman and finding a changeling with butter-coloured hair in his place, she halted, baffled.

"Mr. Lehman?" she said, looking about her. "I came to see Mr. Lehman."

"He'll be back soon, Miss Whittaker," said Dinty.

"What did he want to go out for? I told him I was coming back, and it's important."

A consciousness of his new responsibilities roused Barmy from the stupor into which he had fallen.

"Er—is it something to do with the firm?" he said, and wondered if he should have added 'Sweetheart or 'My blossom'. The technique of being a theatrical manager took some getting into.

"I beg your pardon?"

"I mean to say, if it's something to do with the firm, I could do it, what?"

A questioning graciousness softened the grim intensity of Miss Whittaker's manner.

"I wonder if this is the . . . Mr. Lehman spoke of someone who was coming into the company. . . . Are you——?"

"That's right. I'm a partner."

"Then of *course* you can do it," said Miss Whittaker, letting loose her full battery of charm. "I don't believe Mr. Lehman mentioned your name."

"Phipps."

"I'm Gladys Whittaker, Mr. Phipps. I'm in the show. You're coming to rehearsals soon, aren't you, Mr. Phipps? I'm sure we all want to get your ideas. And I do especially. I'm sure you'll be wonderful. I can't tell you how relieved I am that you've come to take charge of things. Oh, I knew there was something, Mr. Phipps," she said, breaking off as if at some sudden recollection. "I wonder if you would do me a very great favour. I don't like to trouble you, but I left my cheque-book at home this morning, and just now I saw the darlingest little dress, and they won't hold it for poor me," said Miss Whittaker, skirting for one terrible second the edge of baby talk.

Barmy produced his cheque-book.

"Why, of course. How much?"

"A hundred. Make it cash."

"Right ho."

"Thank you," said Miss Whittaker, taking the cheque and bestowing it in her ornate bag. "That's just fine. I think it's wonderful, your coming in with us, Mr. Phipps. It makes everything seem different. Now don't forget. You're coming to rehearsals and you're going to tell me just what you think. If you don't like the way I'm doing something, you'll mention it, won't you?"

"Sure you won't mind?"

"*Mind?*" said Miss Whittaker in a sort of ecstasy. "The one thing a genuine artist wants is advice. Good-bye, Mr. Phipps, and thank you again. Such a pleasure to be under your management."

The door closed. Barmy gaped at it limply. He had found Miss Whittaker, coming on top of that emotional scene, a little overpowering.

Dinty was regarding him with new interest.

"So that's who you are! The angel!"

"Eh?"

"Mr. Lehman was telling me all about you. Have you put money in the show?"

"Eh? Oh, yes, I bunged in a certain sum."

"Well, well. I've often wondered how it would feel to be able to do that. It must be fun being an angel. If I had all the money in the world, like you, I think I'd risk it."

Her choice of verbs brought to life the qualms and tremors which had never wholly left Barmy since that disturbing scene with the loco Mrs. Lehman. He quivered as if some hidden hand had thrust a bare bodkin through the seat of his chair.

"Risk it? You don't think it's risky, do you?"

"Well, plays are always a toss-up, aren't they?"

"But this one. With Mervyn Potter starring."

"Yes of course, his name will be a big draw. But——"

"But what?"

"He's terribly erratic. He might let you down somehow."

"How?"

"I don't know. Somehow. Have you ever met him?"

"Oh, rather. We're great pals. He was at Skeewassett, at the hotel. He was the fellow I was telling you about, the one I saved from being cooked to a crisp. He had set his bungalow on fire, and I happened to spot the conflagration from my window and nipped across and extracted him."

"Well, there you are. He set his bungalow on fire. That's the sort of thing he does. I suppose he had been drinking."

"He was a mite polluted, I fancy."

"They tell me he generally is."

"He certainly was last night. He got us chucked out of the Piazza."

"Well, that's what I mean. Don't you think you're taking rather a chance, putting money in a show where the star drinks?"

Barmy fingered his tie. His jaw had fallen.

"I don't know if you know it, my dear old goddess in human shape, but you're making my flesh creep," he said.

Dinty apologized.

"I'm sorry. I don't want to cast a gloom on the proceedings. Probably everything will be all right."

"It will. I've just remembered that Potter's fiancée has made him go on the wagon. So we shan't have any trouble from that source."

"Well, that's fine."

"And the play's good, what? I mean medium-brow and full of action and what not. It'll be a hit, don't you think?"

"Oh sure. But——"

"You keep saying But."

"I hope it will be a hit. But shows do flop, don't they?"

Barmy, who had risen agitatedly, sank back into his chair. He had paled beneath the tan which a summer in Sunny Maine had given him.

"You mean you think this one will?"

"I'm not saying that. I'm only saying it's a contingency, if that's the word, that you have to budget for. You do get an occasional flop, you know, in the course of the theatrical season. Probably Mr. Potter's name will put the thing over, but accidents do happen. Still, what does it matter to you? You're a millionaire."

"Me?"

"Mr. Lehman said you were."

"I'm not a millionaire. I've got twenty-two thousand dollars."

"What!"

"And eighteen cents."

A hideous suspicion flashed into Dinty's mind.

"You didn't give it all to Mr. Lehman?"

"Good Lord, no. Only ten thousand."

"Oh!"

"What's the matter?"

Dinty was looking like a mother hearing bad news from her idiot child.

"No wonder you asked me to call you Barmy!" Her manner became urgent. "Do you know what you've got to do?"

"What?"

"Phone your bank and stop that cheque before Mr. Lehman can get there and cash it."

"Eh?"

"If there's time."

"But if I do, I shall never see you again."

"Why not?"

"Because I shan't be working here. I was going to work here, with you at my elbow, so to speak. Lord love a duck, that's what made me go into it. That was the whole idea. I had practically decided to give the thing a miss, when you came sailing in. I ascertained that you were permanently on the premises and immediately signed on the dotted line. I wanted to have you at my elbow."

"Well, that was very nice of you. But——"

"You do keep saying But, don't you?"

"You must get out of it."

"But . . . now you've got me saying it . . but how about seeing you again?"

"You'll see me again, all right. I wouldn't let you go out of my life for a million. You can come and take me to lunch."

"Every day?"

"If you want to. And on Sundays we'll go and feed the bears in the Bronx Park Zoo. Now get on that phone, quick. Which is your bank?"

"The Guaranty Trust, Fifth Avenue and Forty-Third Street."

"Oh, heavens! You would pick that one, wouldn't you? The only bank in New York that stays open till four o'clock. I was hoping it was some nice uptown place that closed at three and would be shut when they got there. Hurry, hurry, hurry!"

As Barmy fumbled through the telephone directory, Dinty sat looking at him thoughtfully. She was feeling a little breathless. It was a novel experience to have to regard herself in the role of a *femme fatale*. Like most pretty girls, she had always had a reasonably good opinion of herself, but it had never occurred to her before that there might come into her life men who would count half their fortune well lost in exchange for a smile from her. She felt complimented and gratified. Barmy had ceased to be merely a pleasant young man and had become something portentous. She found that her heart was beating rapidly and that there was a mist before her eyes.

"Oh, gosh!" she cried, as she saw through the mist that the portentous young man had dropped the telephone directory and was groping for it under the desk. Impatience became her dominant emotion.

"Sorry," said Barmy.

"Is this the time to be practising your juggling?"

"It slipped," Barmy explained.

He started to scramble out apologetically and, as he did so, the door opened. Mervyn Potter sauntered in.

"Ah, Phipps," said Mervyn Potter. "You again? Stap my vitals, your ubiquitousness is simply uncanny. Is there no place where you're not? Next time I take a bath, I shall examine the soap dish very carefully to make sure you are not snuggled up in it."

"Oh, hullo, Potter."

"Potter it is, Phipps. First, last and all the time, Potter. So you're taking it easy under the desk for awhile, are you? What a versatile chap you are. Now up trees, now under desks. Tell me, Phipps," said Mervyn Potter, taking the telephone directory and flinging it with a careless gesture into a distant corner, for it was foreign to his policy to allow men to whom he was addressing his conversation to let their attention wander to telephone directories, "do you notice anything about me?"

"Eh?"

"My bursting health," said Mervyn Potter. "My rosy cheeks. That indefinable air of *bien être*. It all comes from being on the wagon. There's nothing like it. I feel like a new man. But what are you doing here, Phipps? Have you taken my advice and come to see Lehman on business?"

Barmy, who had chased the telephone directory like a retriever, came back with it.

"Eh? Yes, I'm a partner."

"You are?"

"You are not," said Dinty. "Get on that phone."

The telephone rang. Mervyn Potter took up the receiver.

"Hello?" he said. "Yes, speaking. What? All right? Of course it's all right. I'm surprised at you for asking such a question." He replaced the receiver. "For you," he said to Barmy. "Your bank. Wanted to know if it was all right to cash a cheque of yours for a paltry ten thousand dollars or some such sum. I said of course it was. Good heavens, if the stability of the bank balance of a

Fotheringay-Phipps is to be questioned by some wretched paying teller probably with watery eyes and spots on his face, things have come to a pretty pass. If that sort of thing is to be allowed to go on, then let the sun be darkened and the moon turned to blood. Hoity-toity, what next?" said Mervyn Potter, summing up.

★ 12 ★

WHEN the late Algernon Swinburne, in his poem *The Garden of Proserpine*, made the statement that even the weariest river winds somewhere safe to sea, he probably had in mind the fact that, though at times it seemed unlikely, the rehearsals of a play do eventually come to an end and that the company does at long last find itself in New Haven, Boston, Philadelphia, or, as in the case of the one partly financed by Barmy Fotheringay-Phipps, in Syracuse.

After four weeks of blood, toil, tears and sweat, the management, director, star, subsidiary actors and camp followers of the Lehmac production *Sacrifice* were distributed about that thriving town, the minor members of the troupe in boarding-houses, the big shots at the Mayflower Hotel.

Barmy, as the man who had made the production possible, had been favoured with ample quarters, Room 726, which had two windows and three armchairs, and already he had made his presence felt. Downstairs in his office Oscar Fritchie, the assistant manager of the hotel, was giving his final riding orders to the waiter who at the conclusion of the opening performance would serve the celebration supper which Barmy had ordered, a supper which was to feature chicken *à la king* and lots of champagne. 'Well iced,' said Oscar Fritchie, and the waiter said 'Sure'. The word Yah had not penetrated to Syracuse.

During the days which had followed his entry into the firm, Barmy had run what is known as the gamut of the emotions, now soaring to the heights, now sinking into the depths. Sometimes the play had looked to him the wow Mr. Lehman had said it was, sometimes it had seemed to justify the trenchant criticism of Mrs. Lehman. Sometimes he had hoped, sometimes despaired. But now, with curtain time approaching, doubts had vanished and he was in a glow of optimism. Last night's dress rehearsal had convinced him. It had gone without a hitch, and it was with a light heart that he was donning the dress clothes which he felt

90

an important Syracuse opening justified. When Mr. Lehman entered, his derby hat on his head, his manner all eager expectancy and good fellowship, he had just finished tying his tie.

"How are you, my blossom?" said Mr. Lehman, then paused, stupefied by the spectacle that met his eyes. "Say!" he ejaculated admiringly, and Jack McClure, who had followed him into the room, expressed the opinion that Barmy looked like Great Lovers Through the Ages.

Barmy felt a twinge of embarrassment. From boyhood up it had been his constant aim to do the done thing, and he sensed criticism in these observations.

"What's the matter?" he said. "Aren't you going to dress?"

"No, but that don't make no difference. How's the kid?"

"I thought—being an opening——"

"Sure. And it's going to be some opening. The biggest Syracuse has ever had."

"Any chance of my having to make a speech, what?"

"I guess not."

"That's good. I didn't really think there was, but just in case I thought I'd put on the old soup and fish."

"Sure. Give 'em an eyeful. What room's Moore in, Jack?"

"Down the way. You want her?"

"Yah. And tell Fanny I'm here in twenty-six."

"Oke," said Jack McClure.

He went out with a last admiring look, and Mr. Lehman explained to what Barmy owed the honour of this visit.

"The reason I come in, my puss, was you got such a fine big room I thought maybe you wouldn't mind if we was to get together up here after the show tonight."

"You mean, to celebrate?"

"Well, sort of talk things over. There might be some changes or something."

"Changes in the play?"

"In case there are any."

Barmy was aware of a slight, but definite, return of the old qualms. He did not like this loose talk about changing the play.

"Isn't it all right?" he asked anxiously.

"Sure, sure. Great. But there might be something, see? Just a line. We'll have to have a conference. I and the wife is cooped up in twenty-eight next door, but this is good and big so we can all get in."

This puzzled Barmy.

"All who?"

"Well, whoever comes. You see, after a show's opened you always have to do some gabbing back and forth. Back and forth and back and forth and so on and so on," said Mr. Lehman, from force of habit. "We'll want to know what everybody thinks, see? I'll tell you what you do. You take a wad of paper at the show tonight and put down everything you see that's wrong. Play, acting, scenery, anything. Make a note of it, and then we'll talk it over."

"What I thought you did after a play has opened is . . . sort of have a spot of supper and celebrate it."

"We can do that, too. Great."

Barmy touched his tie coyly.

"Er—could Miss Moore come?"

"You want her right now?"

"No, to the binge, I meant. There's no objection to her joining the revels, is there?"

"Sure not. You invite her. You'd better tell them downstairs."

"Oh, I did. I saw the assistant manager. His name's Fritchie."

"That screwball!"

"Eh?"

Mr. Lehman's manner became urgent. He might have been a loving father explaining to his adolescent son the facts of life. He had visited Syracuse several times in the course of his career, and the subject of Oscar Fritchie was one on which he held strong opinion.

"You want to watch out for that bird," he said. "Don't let him get near you, or he'll talk your ear off. He's a screwball. He's show-crazy."

"Eh?"

"Off his nut about show business. Give him half a chance and he'll talk your ear off."

"I thought he seemed a nice sort of chap."

"Oh, I've nothing against him, except that if you give him half a chance, he talks your ear off. Keep away from him."

"Right ho."

There was a pause. A grave look had come into Mr. Lehman's rugged face. There was even a suspicion of moisture about his eyes. He held out his hand impulsively.

"Well, sweetheart, tonight's the night. Good luck."

Barmy shook the hand warmly.

"Good luck."

"I just want to say," said Mr. Lehman bluffly, "how swell it's been working with you, Mr. Phipps. I don't think you can ever know, Mr. Phipps, how much your co-operation has meant to all of us. We're all mighty grateful, Mr. Phipps. Thank you."

"Thank *you*," said Barmy. "It's been dashed nice working with you."

"That's the secret of success in the theatre, my blossom," proceeded Mr. Lehman, now visibly affected. "Co-operation. Lots of these shows, something goes wrong on the opening night, and everyone's snarling and snacking at everyone, but we're just one happy family."

"Happy family, that's right."

"And that's what we'll be right along."

"Absolutely."

"Just a happy family."

"Just a happy family."

There was another pause.

"Well, good luck," said Mr. Lehman.

"Good luck," said Barmy.

Silence fell again, as two strong men stood there, wrestling with feelings too deep for utterance. It was broken by the entry of Dinty, followed by Jack McClure.

"Ah!" said Mr. Lehman, discarding sentiment and becoming the man of affairs. "I want you, Moore."

"Here I am, Field-Marshal."

"I want you right beside me during the play, see? Take notes as I dictate 'em. Jack, I just been telling Mr. Phipps what a help he's been to us."

"He certainly has."

"And what a pleasure it was to work with him."

"It certainly was. Good luck, Mr. Phipps."

"Good luck."

"Now there was something, Jack, now what was it?" said Mr. Lehman. "Oh, yes, now here's the angle——"

He led his gentlemanly partner out, talking as he went. Dinty, about to follow, was arrested by a passionate cry.

"Hey!"

"Yes, my pet?"

"Don't go," said Barmy. "I've got something for you."

He blushed to think that, overcome by the emotions surging in his bosom as the result of that tender scene with Mr. Lehman, he had temporarily forgotten it. He went to the cupboard and returned with a large box of flowers. Dinty tottered.

"For me?"

"Yah. I mean Yes. I got them for you for the opening. They're flowers."

"That's what I said to myself, the moment I saw them. Flowers, I said to myself, or my eyes deceive me. How sweet of you, Barmy."

"We Phippses are sweet. We're noted for it all over England."

"You'll make some nice girl a good husband."

"Exactly. And that brings me to the point I wanted to touch on. How many times have I asked you to marry me?"

"I've lost count."

"Well, here I go again. Will you?"

"Oh, Barmy."

"It's no good saying 'Oh, Barmy'."

"What else do you expect me to say?"

"You like me, don't you?"

"Of course I do. Who wouldn't?"

"Well, then."

"If it's no good me saying 'Oh, Barmy', it's certainly no good you saying 'Well, then'."

"Why not?"

Dinty became maternal.

"Because this is a tough world, my child, and we've got to be practical. It isn't just a question of whether I like you or not. I think you're as cute as a little red wagon, but the holy state costs money."

"I've got ten thousand dollars."

"That doesn't last long these days, if you haven't a job."

Barmy found her unintelligible. She seemed to him like a goddess in human shape who was talking through the back of her neck.

"What do you mean, haven't a job? I'm a partner in Lehman Productions, aren't I? And we're going to clean up, aren't we? Listen," said Barmy, inspired. Mr. Lehman's stimulating words at that first meeting had never ceased to remain green in his memory. "Ask Dick Rodgers and Oscar Hammerstein what they're knocking down out of this *South Pacific*. Ask Oscar Serlin what he made out of *Life With Father*. Ask Max Gordon——"

"Yes, I know."

"I'll tell you, my blossom. Millions."

"Yes, I know. But——"

Dinty paused. She had been present at all the rehearsals and they had left her an adherent to the Fanny Lehman school of thought. She had not participated in that emotional scene when Fanny Lehman, speaking of the compact little drama *Sacrifice*, had used the word 'rotten', but if she had been, she would have been obliged to admit that Mr. Lehman's best friend and severest critic had selected the right adjective. She still clung desperately to the hope that a star of Mervyn Potter's eminence, with all the women in America panting to get a sight of him, would be able to put even *Sacrifice* over, but she was exceedingly dubious.

Still, it was not for her to act as a black frost in Barmy's garden of dreams. There might be a bitter awakening, but she was only too happy to see him in this uplifted mood. She put her hands on his shoulders and kissed him, and Barmy shook like a jelly.

"You've never done that before," he said, awed.

"And I wouldn't do it now, if it wasn't that I wanted to wish you luck. That was a mother's kiss."

"Mother's?"

"Mother's," said Dinty firmly. "Don't go getting it mixed up with the kiss of unbridled passion. That'll come later . . . maybe. And why I'm hanging around here, dallying with you and giving you motherly kisses, is more than I know. Mr. Lehman is probably foaming at the mouth. 'She cometh not', he said."

"That's Shakespeare, isn't it?"

"One of those guys. I wouldn't know. They stopped my education before I was full to the brim. Good-bye, Barmy, dear, and good luck. I'm sure everything's going to be fine. And remember, if it isn't perfect tonight, it can probably be fixed. That's what a try-out's for."

"Oh, rather. I'm going to take notes of whatever's wrong."

"That's the way to talk. Up on your toes, boy."

She hurried out, and Barmy, sinking into one of the three armchairs, gave himself up to rapturous meditation, totting up the score to see where he stood.

Things were moving, he considered. She hadn't said Yes, but,

on the other hand, she hadn't said No. She had admitted that
he was not wholly distasteful to her, even going so far as to
state that she found him as cute as a little red wagon. He had no
means of ascertaining how cute this was, but it was apparently
quite fairly cute. And, above all, she had kissed him. A motherly
kiss, she had said, but he wasn't going to believe that.

"Motherly, my foot!" he said aloud, and Gladys Whittaker,
who was entering at the moment, paused and eyed him with not
a little astonishment.

"I beg your pardon?"

Barmy sprang to his feet.

"Oh, hullo. I didn't know you were there. I—er—I was sort
of soliloquizing. Like those blokes in Shakespeare. Er—was
there anything?"

"I was looking for Mr. Lehman."

"He went off to the theatre. Was there something special you
wanted to see him about?"

"Yes," said Miss Whittaker. "There was."

Barmy could now see that there was a peculiar expression on
this substantial blonde's face. A bleak, austere expression. She
was looking more like an aunt than anything human. In his
boyhood he had observed platoons of his aunts with their features
frozen in a similar rigidity. To name but one, his Aunt Charlotte
on the occasion when he had been led into her presence, charged
with having broken the curate's umbrella.

"I want him to speak to Mr. Potter."

Barmy was surprised.

"Isn't he speaking to Potter?" he said. He had heard of no
rift between the two.

"To speak to him seriously. About his drinking."

"Is he *drinking*?" Miss Whittaker looked more like an aunt
than ever. "I am the last person to criticize a fellow artist, Mr.
Phipps, but I feel it my duty to tell you that I saw Mr. Potter
in the lobby just now, and he was stinko."

Barmy reeled.

"Stinko?"

"Stinko," said Miss Whittaker. "I only hope he will be able
to give a performance tonight. Good-bye," she said, and went
out, looking like Cassandra.

Barmy paced the floor in a fever of disquiet and anxiety. Her
words had shaken him to the core. He had so unhesitatingly

accepted Mervyn Potter's statement that he was on the wagon, and it is always disconcerting to find that one has been living in a fool's paradise. At what point the blighter's foot had slipped, causing him to fall from the vehicle, he had no means of ascertaining, but that the fall must have taken place was not to be disputed by the most optimistic. A knowledgeable woman like Miss Whittaker would not have employed the adjective 'stinko', had there been any room for doubt in her mind.

This, he told himself, was a nice bit of box fruit. Of all obstacles to the success of a play, a stinko star is perhaps the most serious. Tales he had heard of curtains being rung down and audiences given their money back came flooding into his mind. Little wonder that he paced the floor.

It was as he turned from pacing it in an easterly direction and was about to pace back toward the west that he saw that he had another visitor.

Reading from left to right, Mervyn Potter.

Barmy's initial emotion on beholding this star to which he had hitched his wagon was a profound relief. Miss Whittaker's gloomy words had left him, as we have seen, a prey to nameless fears, and he had had visions of a whooping, yelling Mervyn Potter, a Mervyn Potter behaving more or less along the lines of Dangerous Dan McGrew shooting up the Malemute saloon. Privileged, that night of the burning bungalow at Skeewassett and again in the grounds of Mrs. C. Hamilton Brimble's mansion at King's Point, Long Island, to observe him when he was going nicely, he knew how animated the Idol of American Womanhood could become in his more relaxed moments. Anticipating a Mervyn Potter who would have to have his head sat on by a posse of strong men while others ran to call out the police reserves, he found the spectacle of him now comforting.

For the Mervyn Potter who came slowly into Room 726 was far from being in the old Skeewassett and King's Point form. His head was bowed, his manner subdued. To all outward appearances, except for a slightly boiled look about the eyes, he might have been a teetotaller who had just received bad news from home.

"Ah, Phipps," he said, in a low, toneless voice, like a spirit whispering into a trumpet at a *séance*.

Barmy became managerial. No theatrical manager likes to see his star loitering in hotel bedrooms with the curtain due to go up at any moment.

"I say!" he said. "Aren't you dressed?"

"What's missing?" said Mervyn Potter, still in that same toneless voice, squinting a lack-lustre eye down at his costume.

"I mean, aren't you going to dress? The show will be starting soon."

"Never mind the show," said Mervyn Potter, becoming more animated. "You leave the show alone, and it'll leave you alone.

I have something serious to say to you, Phipps. As the Walrus said, the time has come to speak of many things."

He lowered himself into an armchair, and after seeming to experience a difficulty in getting him into focus stared owlishly at Barmy.

"Phipps," he said, "we are old friends." He paused, and looked questioningly at Barmy from under his eyebrows. "Aren't we old friends, old friend?"

"Oh, rather."

"Don't qualify it with any 'Oh, rathers'," said Mervyn Potter with a touch of that sternness which had come into his manner on the occasion when Barmy had suggested going off and having dinner. "Either a man is an old friend or he is not an old friend. There is no middle course. You and I, Phipps, are very old friends. I will go further, extremely old friends. Through every peril, every adversity, in fair weather and foul, we two have stood shoulder to shoulder. Like the Boys of the Old Brigade. Are you familiar with the habits of the Boys of the Old Brigade?"

"Eh? No, I don't think I am."

"They stood shoulder to shoulder, and, though I would not tell this to everyone, steadily blade by blade," said Mervyn Potter, and fell into a light sleep. And there the scene might have concluded, had not Barmy, who had begun to pace the floor again, tripped over his visitor's feet.

Mervyn Potter opened his eyes.

"Where were we?" he asked.

"Eh?"

"We were discussing some subject replete, as I recall, with interest. What was it?"

"You were saying that we were old friends."

"So I was. And so we are. You don't dispute that?"

"Oh, no, rather not."

"I should be hurt and disappointed if you did. People sometimes come to me and say 'Tell me, Potter', addressing me, you understand. My name is Potter. 'Tell me, Potter, to settle a bet, are you and Phipps old friends?' and I reply, 'Yes, Griggs or Freylinghausen or whatever the name may be, you are perfectly correct. Phipps and I are excessively old friends. Some friends are young friends, but Phipps and I are old ones. Who ran to help me when I fell and would some pretty story tell and kiss the place to make it well? Phipps. Between Phipps and myself,'

I tell these people, 'there exists a perfect trust and confidence, so that we are able to speak our minds to each other frankly and openly and without offence. If, for example, prompted by the thought of our old friendship, I find myself compelled to talk to Phipps like a kindly elder brother, pointing out that he is hovering on the brink of a precipice, Phipps takes it in good part.' Don't you, Phipps?"

"Oh, definitely."

"No umbrage?"

"None."

"Good. Then I will talk to you like a kindly elder brother now. Phipps, as I was coming along the corridor, I saw that secretary of Lehman's, young Dinty Moore, leaving your room, the inference being that at some earlier point she had sneaked into it. I dozed off for a moment or two, leaning against the wall, and when I opened my eyes, I saw Gladys Whittaker leaving your room, the inference again being that she had previously entered it. How many other females of the species entered your room during the interval when I was taking my siesta, I cannot say. Even now, for all I know, there may be women in every nook and cranny, hiding under the bed, tucked away in closets, peeping out from behind armchairs and nestling in the bath tub. I don't like it, Phipps. I don't like it, old friend. You may try to argue that your heart is young and that you are merely following in the footsteps of Casanova and Charles the Second, but I repeat I do not like it. Cut women out of your life, Phipps, and you will be a better, brighter man. It is the secret of a happy and prosperous career."

Having said which, Mervyn Potter fell asleep again.

Barmy looked at him, bewildered. The sentiments he had just heard expressed were the last he would have expected from one who in previous conversations had always exhibited a rather noticeable enthusiasm for the other sex. He was still seeking vainly for a solution of this *volte face*, when Mervyn Potter woke up and immediately began where he had left off.

"What mighty ills have not been done by Women! Who was't betrayed the Capitol? A woman. Who lost Mark Antony the world? A woman. Who was the cause of a long ten years' war and laid at last old Troy in ashes? Woman. A sex I strongly disapprove of," said Mervyn Potter severely, and added that there ought to be a law.

Barmy's bewilderment increased.

"I thought you liked women."

"No longer, Phipps. Not any more. There was a time when my heart was an open house with Welcome on the mat, but now that heart is broken, Phipps, into a thousand pieces. It has become a crumbling ruin, through the cracks in which the chill winds of despair and disillusionment blow like nobody's business. A woman has done me dirt, Phipps. She has proved as false as she was fair. I allude to my fiancée. Or, rather, my ex-fiancée."

"Well, I'll be blowed. Is she ex?"

"Ex to the last drop. You never saw anything Ex-er. By this morning's mail I received a letter from her, handed in at Nassau in the Bahamas, severing diplomatic relations and giving me the heave-ho in no uncertain terms. Yes, Phipps, she has thrown me out on my little pink behind, and life has become a blank. From sport to sport they hurry me, to stifle my regret, and when they win a smile from me, they think that I forget. But do I, Phipps? No, Phipps, I do not. Not that I've had much time to so far, of course," said Mervyn Potter reasonably.

Barmy sought for words to comfort this broken man.

"I say, I'm frightfully sorry."

"Thank you, Phipps." Mervyn Potter thrust out a hand to clasp Barmy's, missed it by about two feet six inches, over-balanced, fell, picked himself up with an encouraging 'Upsy-daisy' and resumed. "Your sympathy touches me. I don't say it mends my broken heart, but it touches me. Thank you, old friend. Well, that's how matters stand. I pray you, in your letters, Phipps, when you shall these unlucky deeds relate, speak of me as I am; nothing extenuate, nor set down aught in malice. Then must you speak of one who loved not wisely but too well . . . You haven't got a drop of whisky anywhere, have you?" said Mervyn Potter, changing the subject.

"I'm afraid I haven't."

"Scotch? Rye? Bourbon? I'm not particular."

"I'm afraid nót."

"Ah, well. That's Life, isn't it?"

"But what on earth happened?"

Mervyn Potter brooded for a moment.

"It is a long, sad story, throwing a blinding light on Woman's treachery and general skulduggery. Do you know what that girl did, Phipps? No, don't tell me, I'll tell you. Throw your mind back to that night when we dropped in at the Brimble residence, and you climbed all those trees. Do you recall my telling you that she bade me cut out all alcoholic stimulants?"

"Yes, I remember. You did it, didn't you?"

Mervyn Potter heaved a heavy sigh.

"I did. I kept my trust faithfully and well. She had a way of sniffing at me suddenly which rendered any other course impossible. For three long, weary weeks nothing passed my lips but barley water and an occasional lemonade. And then what happened? In company with her father, C. Hamilton Brimble of King's Point, Long Island, and her mother, Mrs. C. Hamilton Brimble, oddly enough also of King's Point, Long Island, she went off to Nassau for a change of air, leaving me alone . . . alone in New York."

Mervyn Potter sighed again, even more heavily than before. It was plain that whatever the story was that he was about to relate, it was one that racked him to his foundations, and Barmy felt a pang of pity. He also felt a cold tremor down his spine as he snatched a surreptitious glance at his watch and read the position of its hands. Long ere this the stricken man should have been in his dressing-room, slapping on the grease paint.

"The parting," resumed Mervyn Potter, "was agony. I felt like one of those fellows in the early nineteenth-century poems who used to go around losing dear gazelles. Still, in every cloud wrack the experienced eye, if it peers closely enough, can detect some sort of a silver lining, and the horror of my predicament was mitigated by the reflection that, now that she was no longer there to sniff suddenly at me, I would be able to start ingurgitating once more. The man of honour," said Mervyn Potter, putting in a nutshell his philosophy of life, "keeps his word to the woman he loves while she's around. When she's not around, conditions alter. To cut a long story short, Phipps, she was scarcely on the boat when I proceeded to line up at the Lambs Club bar with all the enthusiasm of a camel which, after toiling for days through the hot sands, finds itself at an oasis. I also lubricated the system at many a restaurant and night club. I had leeway to make up, and I made it up."

"And she found out?"

Mervyn Potter sighed for the third time, the sigh of a man who has drunk life's bitter wine to the lees and whose faith in woman is dead.

"How could she help but find out, old friend? You would scarcely believe that a pure-minded girl, a product of Miss Finch's school and Vassar University, could be capable of such a thing, but before leaving for Nassau she had put herself in touch with the Day and Night Detective Agency, and my every move, though I did not know it, was being closely followed by Private Eyes complete with book and pencil. They tailed me up, Phipps, making copious notes, and handed in their report to Heloise, only daughter of C. Hamilton Brimble (and, of course, Mrs. C. Hamilton Brimble) of King's Point, Long Island, with the results which you now see before you. So there you have the whole story. Well, good-bye, Phipps, old friend. I must not trespass on your time. No doubt you have a hundred things to do."

"And you'll be getting along to the theatre, what?"

Mervyn Potter stared.

"Theatre?"

"It's awfully late."

"Theatre?" said Mervyn Potter, amazed. "Getting along to the theatre? I'm not going to any theatre. They'll have to put my understudy on. Good heavens, Phipps, you don't seriously suppose that I could play an exacting part, handicapped by this broken heart of mine? I'm going to have another drink or two and then go off and join the Foreign Legion, that cohort of the damned where broken men toil and die and, dying, forget. Good-bye, Phipps," said Mervyn Potter, and with a kindly word of warning to his old friend not to take any wooden nickels, walked heavily from the room, dragging his feet and giving little jumps from time to time, as though vultures were gnawing at his bosom.

★ 14 ★

IF the Lithuanian chambermaid who at half-past nine that night came to turn Barmy's bed down had been at all psychic—which, of course, very few Lithuanian chambermaids are—she would have sensed, as she went about her work, a strange, almost eerie atmosphere in Room 726, as of a room in a haunted house that is waiting for its spectre to clock in and start haunting. It is an atmosphere which always clings about those hotel apartments in New Haven, Syracuse and other try-out towns where before long haggard men will be meeting to conduct the post-mortem on a newly opened play. It was as though Room 726 were holding its breath, anticipating it knew not what.

From nine-thirty till shortly after eleven it continued in this painful state of suspense. Then a key clicked in the lock, and Barmy entered, whistling gaily. Leaving the door open behind him, he switched the lights on and advanced into the room, still whistling, his whole aspect such as to create the impression that he had found the blue bird. A spectre, had one been present, would have recognized him at a glance as a young man, financially interested in a theatrical production, who had just witnessed that theatrical production laying them in the aisles and massacring them, and would probably have resolved to dig down into its ectoplasm for the price of a ticket.

A few moments later, however, it would have found itself changing its mind and deciding to keep the money in the old winding-sheet. For it was now that Joseph Lehman made his appearance, and there was that about Mr. Lehman's manner which would have chilled the spine of the stoutest spectre. Followed at a respectful distance by a dejected Jack McClure, he looked like someone who has come to lay a wreath on the tomb of an old friend. His back was bowed, his eyes cast down. He still wore his derby hat, but even that had lost its jaunty tilt and seemed to droop on its stem. With a sigh that came up from the soles of his feet, he sank heavily on to the bed, while

Jack McClure, with a similar sigh, slumped into a chair.

Barmy regarded the two mourners with bewilderment. Tonight of all nights he wanted to see smiling faces about him, and judging from their appearance and behaviour it looked as though, like a famous English king, Joseph Lehman and Jack McClure would never smile again. It puzzled him. Easily pleased as a theatre-goer, it had seemed to him that the performance which had just concluded had gone with a swing. For the first time, he began to entertain doubts. Gloom like this was surely not the usual thing after a first night success.

"I say," he said. "Is something the matter?"

He received no reply. Mr. Lehman was picking at the coverlet, Jack McClure drumming on the arm of his chair. He tried again.

"I thought it went awfully well, what?" he said. Then, observing Mr. Lehman's convulsive start and seeing Jack McClure's head jerk back as if someone had struck him between the eyes, he qualified the statement a trifle. "Well, except here and there, I mean to say. In spots, as it were."

Again neither of his two business colleagues spoke. It was as though they had taken Trappist vows, and his uneasiness deepened. He was not, as has been indicated, a highly intelligent young man, but even he could see that there was a possibility that he had been mistaken in supposing that all was for the best in the best of all possible worlds. He was still trying to correct a growing disposition to shake like a blancmange, when he heard a cough, one of those dry, unpleasant coughs, and perceived Mrs. Lehman sailing in like a battleship going into action.

"Oh, hullo," he said. "What ho, there."

Fanny, her eyes fixed on Mr. Lehman, ignored the greeting. She was fond of Barmy and generally enjoyed chatting with him, but she was busy now arranging her thoughts preparatory to addressing her husband. Victory was so completely hers that she hardly felt that words were necessary. Nevertheless, she proposed to speak a few. She came well into the room, picked a prominent spot and settled herself to begin.

"*First!*" said Fanny.

Life returned to Mr. Lehman's rigid limbs. He sprang to his feet.

"Now one thing we ain't going to have none of is wisecracks," he thundered. " Get me?"

Fanny laughed. A light, tinkling laugh.

"You could have used a few wisecracks in that charade tonight," she said. "Yessir, you could have used lantern slides. You could have used acrobats and performing dogs."

"Now, listen——"

"*And* trained seals," said Fanny.

Mr. Lehman's hat quivered.

"Does that trap of yours ever close?" he inquired with strained politeness.

"From time to time."

"Then close it now," urged Mr. Lehman. "I don't want to hear no more of all that. They can't nobody tell me we ain't got a great show . . . when it's fixed. Just because this bunch tonight didn't like it don't prove nothing. Syracuse is the worst show town in America."

This news surprised Barmy, who had been told otherwise.

"I thought you said——"

"Never mind what I said. Shut up."

"Oh, right ho. Still, you did remark——"

"Shut *up*, I tell you."

Barmy subsided, his feelings wounded. Was this, he was asking himself, the man who had clasped his hand and, with tears as near as a toucher in his eyes, thanked him for his co-operation and told him how swell it had been working with him? His limited acquaintance with the theatre had not yet taught him that between the demeanour of a manager on the even of a production and that of the same manager immediately after the failure of that production there is a subtle but well-marked difference, generally more well-marked than subtle.

Mr. Lehman resumed his remarks.

"If it didn't go just right tonight, what of it? What can you expect when your star walks out on you half an hour before the opening and you have to put on a lousy understudy?"

Fanny would have none of this specious reasoning.

"Don't talk to me about lousy understudies. That guy Spender gave a dam sight better performance than Mervyn Potter would ever have done. It's the play that's wrong."

"What's wrong with it?"

"Let me tell you," said Fanny, licking her lips. "*First!*"

It was perhaps fortunate, for Mr. Lehman was a man with a high blood pressure, that at this moment there was an interruption. A waiter entered, bearing a folding table and other supper accessories. He was short and stout and probably the friendliest waiter in Syracuse.

"This where the party's going to be, folks?" he asked genially.

Barmy came out of his reverie.

"Oh, thanks. Yes, right ho," he said. He turned to Mr. Lehman. His feelings were still hurt, but one must overcome wounded feelings at a time like this. "I say, it's just a little thing, isn't it, what? The matter, I mean? I mean to say, the play's a success, isn't it?"

Mr. Lehman gave him a long, lingering look, but did not speak. The waiter unfolded the folding table.

"Mr. Fritchie says he'll be up later to see if everything's all right," he said, and Mr. Lehman quivered like a harpooned whale.

"All I need is that screwball!" he moaned. "Get out!"

"Yes, sir."

"Fritchie!" said Mr. Lehman. The way he spoke the name made it sound like one of those robust Elizabethan oaths, the sort of thing rare Ben Jonson in a testy moment might have flung at Beaumont and Fletcher over the sherris sack in the Mermaid Tavern. "At a time like this . . . Fritchie!"

Silence fell once more on Room 726. It was broken by Fanny.

"I wonder if I might ask a question?" she said with a meek sweetness which affected Mr. Lehman like the touch of a red-hot poker. He leaped feverishly, his hat swaying.

"Lay off!" he urged. "Lay off me, I'm telling you."

Fanny was not to be diverted. It was her duty to be helpful, and helpful she intended to be.

"I was only going to ask if you were planning to put anything in that five-minute spot where Whittaker couldn't think of the next line," she said, all gentle wifely solicitude. "Because if she's going to wait like that every night, I figure it would be a great place for a specialty. A ballet of some kind. Or I could come on with the clubs——"

"Lay off!" said Mr. Lehman, fermenting visibly. "Lay off, lay off, lay off!"

"We're all working for the good of the show," said Fanny virtuously. "There's a troupe of Swiss bellringers I saw at——"

"Will you stop it!" roared Mr. Lehman. He turned to Jack McClure. "Did you tell that director we was meeting here?"

"Be here any minute."

"How about Bernie?"

"I give him the room."

"And where's Moore with those notes of mine?"

Barmy became helpful.

"Here are my notes, Mr. Lehman, if you would care to——"

"Better give Bernie a ring. Get him up here."

"Right," said Jack McClure. "I didn't see him at the show."

"I saw him," said Fanny.

"What did he say?" asked Mr. Lehman. "Don't tell me," he added quickly, as he observed his wife's face light up.

Barmy was still persevering.

"Here are the notes I bunged down, Mr. Lehman, if you would care to take a dekko. There's one with ref. to the orchard scene which I am particularly anxious to draw to your——"

"Ah!" said Mr. Lehman.

Dinty Moore had come in, bringing with her the script of the play, an ample sheaf of Mr. Lehman's obiter dicta and an assortment of well-sharpened pencils. Her manner was subdued, lacking all trace of its customary brightness. She looked like one of those characters in ghost stories who have seen some awful sight, as of course she had. Barmy's welcoming 'What ho' brought no answering smile to her lips. Nice girls do not smile at funerals.

"Gimme them notes," said Mr. Lehman, seating himself at the writing-table. "Gimme the script. Gimme a pencil."

"Gimme Mr. Sampson, Kitty," said Jack McClure at the telephone. "He's in four-thirteen. Oh, say, how did you like the show, Kitty?"

"Now then," said Mr. Lehman, opening the script.

"Oh?" Jack McClure's exclamation was one of pain. It was evident that he had received a none too cheering reply from the lady at the switchboard. "Well, I wouldn't go as far as that," he said, having winced a little. "You got to understand it's still new yet. It needs work, of course. But by the time we hit the big town it'll be clicking all along the line."

"Ah!" said Barmy, encouraged. This, he felt, was more the old bulldog spirit.

Mr. Lehman motioned Dinty to the chair at his side.

"Now you take down anything that comes up, see? And I don't want . . . Oh, my God, he's in again!"

The waiter had returned, this time laden with bottles of champagne. Fanny's eyes followed him bulgingly as he crossed the room.

"Well!" said Fanny, lost in admiration of this lavishness. "Your birthday?"

"Eh?" said Barmy. "Oh, it's to celebrate the success of the play."

Fanny's eyebrows rose.

"The what of the which?"

"The success of the play,"

"I thought that was what you said." Fanny walked across and took up a bottle. "Do they open?"

"Oh, rather."

"Soon?"

"Oh, I see what you mean. Waiter, will you open a bot or two?"

"Pardon me for seeming in a hurry," said Fanny, "but you see I saw all three acts."

Jack McClure, at the telephone, had established communication with the mysterious Bernie.

"Bernie? Mac."

"Tell him to hurry up," said Mr. Lehman, chafing.

"We're getting together up here in 726, Bernie, whenever you're ready," said Jack McClure. "Okay."

He hung up. The waiter was lingering in the doorway.

"Mr. Fritchie says how soon do you want the food served?"

"Oh, yes," said Barmy, recalled to his duties as a host. "Would you like the garbage lugged in right away?"

"I don't care," said Mr. Lehman, his mind still above mundane matters. "All I ask is keep that Fritchie away from here."

"You wish to see Mr. Fritchie?" said the waiter brightly.

"No, I don't wish to see Mr. Fritchie. Scram!"

"Yes, sir. Remember what MacArthur told the Japanese when they pushed him out of the Philippines?"

"No."

" 'I shall return'," said the waiter.

Two measures of champagne had given Fanny the party spirit. She proposed a jolly toast.

"To Gladys Whittaker, queen of the deaf mutes!" she said, raising her glass.

Mr. Lehman banged on the table.

"Shut that door!" he bellowed. "And where is everybody? I pay a director the earth. Where is he? I bring Bernie Sampson up from New York. Where is he? Aren't I ever to get no co-operation? Ah!" said Mr. Lehman. "And about time."

Cecil Benham, the director, was coming into the room.

★ 15 ★

CECIL BENHAM was calm, reserved, well stricken in years and very dignified. There were those, though Mr. Benham was not among them, who considered him a fossil, a back number and an anachronism. He had been at his best as a director many years ago in the great days of the New York stage, when motion pictures were in their infancy and Television a horror still in the mists of the future. As he came placidly into the room, giving the impression, though this was not actually so, that he had a scarlet-lined opera cape about his shoulders, he brought with him something of the atmosphere of those spacious times.

Many men, meeting Cecil Benham, felt a sort of nostalgic reverence, as if they were in the presence of some noble old public monument. Mr. Lehman did not belong to this group.

"Hey!" he barked, getting right down to it without wasting time on courteous preliminaries. "What happened to that scenery?"

Mr. Benham gave him the calm, dignified look which he might have given a bumptious young actor at the Players' Club.

"I beg your pardon?"

"I said, what happened to the scenery? It was crooked, all through the show."

"That was one of the things I bunged down," said Barmy, helpful as ever, "particularly with ref. to the orchard scene. I don't know if you happen to know it, but in a real orchard——"

Cecil Benham's calm was disturbed by the faintest suggestion of annoyance.

"My dear Mr. Lehman, I was hardly in a position to prevent that. A director cannot be everywhere. I was holding book all the evening."

"Well, if you were holding book, where were you during that stage wait of Whittaker's in the second act? Couldn't you give her the line?"

"I gave Miss Whittaker the line four times, but it

111

appeared to make no impression on her. She seemed nervous."

Barmy had light to throw on this.

"She wasn't feeling well, poor soul."

"What?"

"So she told me."

"When did you see her?"

"In her dressing-room after the first act. I was giving her some suggestions."

"*You* were?"

"That's right. I was telling her that in the big scene with the hero in the bedroom she ought to do some of her best acting, really pull up her socks, don't you know."

Mr. Lehman swelled. He looked like a minor prophet of the Old Testament about to curse the people for their sins.

"Well, for——"

He broke off. There had come a knock on the door. Barmy was in the fortunate position of a pugilist who has been saved by the bell.

"Come in," shouted Mr. Lehman.

"Maybe it's Bernie," said Jack McClure.

It was Bernie, and not only Bernie, but a young lady.

Bernie Sampson was a sallow young man who wore that air of desiccated sophistication which can be acquired only through long service on Broadway. He was what is known in theatrical circles as a fixer. Once, several years before, he had made a suggestion for the improvement of a comedy which was in its death agony out of town. The suggestion was misunderstood by the producer, and the mistaken suggestion saved the play. Ever since then Bernie Sampson had been a recognized dramatic doctor. A sort of vulture hovering over the theatrical scene, he had witnessed a vast number of plays open and close, and with each one he had participated in just such a bedroom conference as this.

As for the young lady whom he was escorting, her name was Peggy Marlowe, and she was not unknown to the choruses of Broadway. It was her custom to appear for about a month in one of the most prominent musical comedies of the town and then to desert abruptly for Florida. She was smartly dressed and extremely good-looking.

"Hello, people," said Bernie, tossing his hat on to the bed. "Hello, Joe. How are you, Mackie?" He waved a hand in the direction of Peggy. "I just happened to have a young lady with me. This is Miss Marlowe, folks."

"How are you?" said Miss Marlowe, blowing a cloud of smoke from the long cigarette-holder which was as permanent a decoration of her shapely lips as was Mr. Lehman's derby hat of Mr. Lehman's head.

Jack McClure did the honours.

"Mrs. Lehman . . . Mr. Benham . . . and Mr. Phipps."

"Pleased to meet you, Mrs. Lehman. Hey, Mr. Benham. Hi, Mr. Phipps. Ah, mucilage," said Bernie, sighting the champagne.

Mr. Lehman stuck doggedly to the agenda. He frowned at the champagne, holding the view that it struck a frivolous note out of keeping with the solemnity of the occasion.

"Now, Bernie, I want you to tell us just what you think of it. Mr. Sampson here," explained Mr. Lehman, addressing Mr. Benham, "come up from New York to see the show and maybe do some work if it needs it."

"If?" said Fanny. "What do you mean, if?"

"Indeed?" said Cecil Benham, none too pleased. He regarded the fixer with a wary eye. There had been Bernies back in the old days and he had never liked them.

"Now we're all going to give our frank opinions, see?" said Mr. Lehman. "We're going to say just what we thought of the show."

Fanny rose obligingly, a little unsteady on her feet.

"Well," she began. "*First!*"

"That's enough," said Mr. Lehman quickly. "Go ahead, Bernie."

The portentous manner of the seasoned fixer enveloped Bernie Sampson like a garment. He went into his opening speech with the confidence of one who is on familiar ground.

"Well, of course there ain't no doubt but what it needs some work."

"Hard labour," suggested Fanny, busy with the champagne. "If not the death sentence."

"Ah, shut up," said Mr. Lehman.

"Now, when I watch a show," proceeded Bernie profoundly, "I don't look at the show so much, I look at the audience. They'll tell you every time. Now, your Prologue is great. It's a great idea, him reading the play. And it held them. But after that they begin to slip away from you."

"I'd like to ventilate just that point," said Barmy, full of zeal, "with particular ref. to the orchard scene——"

"Who's this?" asked Bernie. "Phipps did you say his name was?"

"That's right," said Barmy. "I'm——"

"If you don't mind, Mr. Phipps——"

"Oh, right ho. I only wanted to say that in the orch——"

He broke off, startled and intimidated by Mr. Lehman's glare. Mr. Lehman allowed his eyes to dwell on him for perhaps ten seconds, then turned to Bernie.

"Yah? You were saying——?"

Mr. Sampson resumed.

"Well, like I'm telling you, it needs work. Some of them scenes, they don't quite click. Now I got a scene that I done in a show called——"

Miss Marlowe's roving eye had discovered Barmy.

"Hello, cutie," she said affectionately.

"Oh, hullo," said Barmy.

"You're English, aren't you?"

"Yah."

"Don't you mean 'Right ho?' Nice hair you've got."

"Oh, thanks."

"Kind of butter-coloured, isn't it?"

"Butter-coloured in spots, no doubt."

"It does something to me," said Miss Marlowe, with that same affectionate note in her voice.

Bernie Sampson had lost the thread of his remarks.

"Say, what goes on here?" he asked suspicously.

"Mind your own business," said Peggy Marlowe.

Mr. Lehman flung his hands heavenwards. His voice shook the ceiling. He had conceived a violent antipathy to Miss Marlowe.

"Bernie, can't you get rid of this beazel?" he pleaded.

"Let him try!" said Miss Marlowe equably. "What I got on him!"

"Are we going to get anything done?" demanded Mr. Lehman, "or aren't we?"

"I vote no," said Fanny.

"What I vote," said Miss Marlowe, "is that somebody slips me a tankard of that juice. I'm surprised you haven't offered me any before, dreamboat," she went on, addressing Barmy reproachfully. "Who do you think I am? Volstead or someone?"

"Give her a glass of that stuff," said Mr. Lehman imperiously, jerking his chin at Barmy and his thumb at the champagne, and Barmy sprang to the task with the alacrity of a man doing a job at which he knows he is good. He was beginning to get the impression that the other members of the conference, notably Mr. Lehman, were bad listeners, but even if he was unable to secure attention for his views, he could pour champagne. He filled Miss Marlowe's glass, and Miss Marlowe drained it and said: 'Boy!'

"Yah?" said Mr. Lehman, having caught Bernie Sampson's eye, which had been showing a tendency to wander in the direction of his young lady. "You was saying you got a scene."

"Yah. You got to put something in the place of that cabaret thing. If ever I seen a Kiss of Death!" said Bernie, shuddering. "Of course," he went on, in the manner of one who looks at a problem from every angle, "it may be the way it was put on. I don't know who done it for you, but of all the lousy directing——!"

Cecil Benham rose to his full height.

"I beg your pardon, Mr. Jackson?"

"Bernie Sampson is my name."

"Indeed? Mine is Cecil Benham."

"Is that so?"

"Possibly you do not know who I am."

"That's only part of it."

"I was associated for ten years with David Belasco. I have directed Nazimova. I have directed Edmund Breeze. I have directed Lowell Sherman, Cyril Scott and Jeanne Eagels."

"And where are they now?" said Fanny, waving her glass.

"And I am not accustomed to having my direction described by the adjective which you have employed."

Bernie Sampson bridled.

"Listen. I come up from New York as a favour to Joe here——"

"Nevertheless, I must insist——"

"Now don't let's get scrapping," pleaded Mr. Lehman.

"But if he is to be permitted——"

"There's no use flying off the handle."

"Yes, but——"

"He didn't mean anything. Just kidding, see? That's the stuff," said Mr. Lehman, as the injured director slowly resumed his seat.

"Is that going to be all?" inquired Miss Marlowe. "Well, call me for the next round," she said, and stretched herself restfully at full length on the bed, ignoring the fact that Mr. Lehman was giving her one of those looks of his which up to the present he had been reserving for Barmy and the partner of his joys and sorrows.

"Go on, Bernie," said Mr. Lehman, with the air of a man of high blood pressure who, following his doctor's recommendation, has just counted ten slowly. "What's this scene you've got?"

"Well, I'll tell you. It'll drop right in where your cabaret is, see? It was a wow scene, but the show never come into New York, so it'll be new. It was a hop joint in Hong Kong."

"It would not possibly do," said Cecil Benham with great dignity.

Even Mr. Lehman seemed a little dubious.

"We got to stick to the story, Bernie. We can't throw away the whole play."

"Why not?" said Fanny.

"What we got to do is start at the beginning . . . Who's this?" said Mr. Lehman, as a knock sounded on the door.

"The police, if there's any law and justice in Syracuse," said Fanny. "Do a dive through the window, I would if I was you. Don't let them take you alive."

"Open that door," said Mr. Lehman.

"Me?" said Barmy.

"Yah."

"Right ho," said Barmy. He had the feeling that all he needed to make him a commissionaire was a peaked cap and the uniform of a Ruritanian admiral, but his was a sweet and obliging disposition, and he had been ordered about by his Uncle Theodore too much in his youth to take offence at a little peremptoriness now.

He went to the door and opened it.

IT was Gladys Whittaker who entered, a Gladys Whittaker plainly in defiant mood and prepared to counter possible attacks on her artistry. She got a round of applause from Fanny, but appeared not to appreciate it. She took up her stand in the precise centre of the room and burst into speech.

"Before anything is said," began Gladys Whittaker in a low, thrilling voice, "the stage wait was not my fault. Mr. Spender gave me the wrong cue, a cue out of the third act. So of course I had to stop and think."

"You certainly had a lovely evening for it," said Fanny sympathetically.

"You'd think there would be someone in the wings to throw me a line. But no."

Cecil Benham swelled ominously. The Benhams did not war on women unless the women asked for it. This he considered, Miss Whittaker was now doing.

"I gave you the line distinctly."

"Well, I didn't hear it."

"That is scarcely my fault."

"Oh, goody!" said Peggy Marlowe, sitting up on the bed. These raised voices promised well for one of those battles of which she was so enthusiastic an *aficionado*.

"I've had a raging headache all day," said Miss Whittaker, her voice quivering with self-pity. "And if you suppose," she went on, suddenly switching her attack to Barmy, "that it is easy for an artist to give a performance of a big part with people coming back into your dressing-room all the time, making idiotic suggestions——"

Barmy felt like Caesar stabbed by Brutus.

"But, dash it all," he cried, aghast at this ingratitude, "you told me you wanted me to make idiotic suggestions . . . I mean——"

"Well, really, Mr. Phipps, I've been longer in the profession than you have——"

117

"And *that's* no fairy tale," said Fanny.

Miss Whittaker drew herself up.

"I beg your pardon?"

"Oh, stop it, you two," bellowed Mr. Lehman. "Now—we're going to begin at the beginning and go right through the show."

Jack McClure had a brain wave.

"Joe, do you want some good straight dope? A fresh viewpoint?"

"Who?"

"There's a little girl down on the switchboard, smart as a steel trap. She sees everything that comes here, and I slipped her a couple tonight."

"Good idea. Get her up. Anybody but that Fritchie."

Miss Marlowe, who had turned on her side and appeared to be about to go to sleep, rolled over and sat up. There was a rather intent look on her face, like that of a leopardess preparing for the kill.

"Did he say on the switchboard?"

"Now, baby," pleaded Bernie. He had heard that note in her voice before.

Jack McClure was talking into the telephone.

"Kitty? This is Mr. McClure. Say, can you leave there for a minute and come up to 726? . . . I'll tell you when you get here. That's right. Good-bye."

Miss Marlowe was still brooding.

"Is there more than one operator in this hotel?"

"Now, baby," said Bernie.

"Because I just had a run in with one of them and I'd like to know."

Mr. Lehman raised his voice.

"Bernie, can't you get this dame to——"

"Some other time, baby."

"Well, just in case she is the one," said Miss Marlowe, "I'll take another drink."

"Now come one," said Mr. Lehman, calling the meeting to order. "We ain't going to have no more interruptions. We're going to take up the scenes as they come along. Now. We're set on the Prologue. Okay?"

"Okay," said Bernie Sampson.

"Okay," said Jack McClure.

"How about you, Benham? Prologue okay?"

"Oh, I am quite satisfied. Perfectly."

"Well, don't get sore about it. Put that down," said Mr. Lehman to Dinty. "Prologue okay."

"Prologue okay," said Barmy, making a gratuitous endorsement, and catching Mr. Lehman's eye dived at the nearest champagne bottle, embarrassed. Odd, he was thinking, not for the first time this evening, how greatly changed the other's manner toward him was tonight. Not the same old hearty friendliness at all. What had become of the big-hearted crony who had so often addressed him as 'my puss' and 'blossom boy'?

Miss Whittaker had a suggestion to offer.

"What's wrong with this play is that the heroine doesn't have sympathy. I'm fighting the audience all the time. I feel it. They don't like me."

Fanny went to all the trouble of getting up.

"Well, I think you were fine. I really do." She resumed her seat. "That'll give you some rough idea of my condition," she said, reaching out for her glass.

Miss Whittaker, after one icy glance, ignored her—as far as it was possible ever to ignore Fanita, the World's Greatest Juggler.

"No sympathy. That's the answer. Something ought to be put in to show that I'm really all right at heart and not just a frivolous Society butterfly."

"How about giving out pamphlets?" said Fanny.

"If I could have a scene early in the play that would show me in a more sympathetic light . . . maybe a scene with a baby."

"We'll come back to it," said Mr. Lehman. "Make a note," he said to Dinty. "Baby for Miss Whittaker."

"Not if it's early in the play, though, what?" said Barmy. "She isn't married."

"All right, all *right*!" There was a knock. "Open that door."

"Me?"

"Yah."

"Right ho," said Barmy.

It was the waiter, laden with chicken *à la king*.

"The chow," announced the waiter cheerily. "I told you I would return."

"Bung it on the table."

"Yes, sir. Come an' get it, folks, come an' get it," said the waiter, with the same chummy air of a kindly soul who wants to make everybody happy.

Mr. Lehman glowered at the chicken *à la king*. Chicken *à la king* meant nothing to Mr. Lehman. He lived only for his art.

"Come on, come on, come on," he shouted. "We can't stop here all night. We're going ahead from the Prologue. The next is the orchard scene."

Barmy's face lit up. This was his big moment.

"I want to say something with ref. to that, Mr. Lehman."

"You don't tell me!"

"I was just waiting till you reached it. You see, my dear old companion——"

"Would you mind letting *me* talk for a minute? And don't call me your old companion."

"Right ho, old egg."

It is possible that Mr. Lehman might have made some comment on this alternative form of address, but at this moment there was another knock on the door, and Barmy, once more directed to open it, found himself confronted by a small girl in a neat black dress, at whom he gazed inquiringly.

"Oh, here's Kitty, Joe," said Jack McClure, supplying the necessary footnotes. "Kitty from the switchboard. This is Miss Humphreys, everybody. Now, here's the angle, Kitty. We want you to tell us just what you thought of the show tonight, see? Straight from the shoulder. You see all the shows that come here. We want to know your real opinion."

Miss Marlowe, seated on the bed, was regarding the newcomer with a speculative eye.

"Well, I'll tell you, Mr. McClure," said Kitty. "You see, Syracuse is a funny town."

"Oh, *that's* it?" said Fanny.

"It's a hard town to please, sort of," proceeded the oracle, speaking the speech of every small-town playgoer, "because you see we get all the new shows. The managers all bring their shows here, because they know if it goes here, it'll go any place. You see, the people here are funny, sort of. If they like a show, they'll go to it, but if they don't like it, they wont."

"That's a hot lot of news," said Mr. Lehman unpleasantly.

"Listen, folks," said the waiter. "I can tell you what's wrong with your show. I wasn't there, but the chambermaid on Number Four was, and she——"

"Just a minute," said Jack McClure. "We want this young lady to——"

"Oh, I beg your pardon," said the waiter. "You have the floor, Miss."

Peggy Marlowe had risen from the bed. Her manner was quiet but menacing.

"Are you the operator that took a New York call out of four-thirteen this evening?" she inquired in a cold, level voice.

"Now, baby," said Bernie.

"Are you?"

"Yes, I am."

"You were pretty fresh, weren't you?"

"I don't think so."

"Well, I do. Are you or are you not supposed to be respectful?"

"I'm always respectful, madam, when I'm speaking to a lady."

There was a pause.

"I'll tell you what you want," said Miss Marlowe, struck with an idea. "You want your ugly little face pushed in."

The words were spoken casually, easily. Peggy Marlowe, veteran of fifty dressing-room fights, was not even mildly excited. Her statement, however, came close to breaking up the meeting. Fanny uttered an encouraging 'Whoopee!'. Mr. Lehman gave a wordless cry. Bernie said 'Now, baby!'. Mr. Benham clicked his tongue and murmured 'Really, really!', and you could see that he was feeling that this sort of thing could never have occurred under the auspices of David Belasco. Jack McClure did the clever, practical thing. In his quiet, gentlemanly way, he pushed Kitty out of the room and closed the door, and there was a moment of complete and grateful calm.

Mr. Lehman was breathing heavily.

"Lock that door!" he said.

"Me?"

"Yah."

"Right ho," said Barmy.

"You'll only have to unlock it again," the waiter pointed out, "to permit me to make an egress. Well, folks, I was going to tell you what this chambermaid said, the one on Number Four. She said to me, 'Rupert,' she said to me, 'what the theatregoer today wants is entertainment'."

Mr. Lehman howled like a banshee.

"Get out!"

"Okay, sir. You're the boss. Good night, folks."

"Good *night*!" said Mr. Lehman.

Barmy was feeling bewildered. This was the first after-opening-performance conference at which he had assisted, and it was completely unlike anything his imagination had pictured. He had envisaged a group of genial people—what Mr. Lehman in a moment of inspiration had so well described as a happy family—exchanging amiable small talk as they sipped their champagne. He had expected something on the lines of one of those eighteenth-century salons of which he had read at school, and he appeared to have been plunged into the middle of a cage of rather exceptionally short-tempered wild cats. It perplexed and confused him. There was nobody to tell him that the current get-together had been, by normal theatrical standards, almost unusually urbane.

Mr. Lehman called the meeting to order once more.

"Come on, now, come on, come on," he said in that forceful way of his. "We're here to decide about this show, and we're getting nowheres."

"I move we make this a permanent organization and meet every week," said Fanny.

"Shut up!"

"I didn't open my mouth."

"Gab, gab, gab . . . We were up to the Prologue."

"Prologue okay," said Barmy sagely.

Mr. Lehman favoured him with another of those incandescent looks. On these occasions when all has not gone well with an opening performance, it is theatrical custom for the presiding manager to select from the little group about him a single individual on whom to expend his fury. Lacking the author who as a rule automatically gets the nomination, Mr. Lehman had chosen Barmy. Barmy, though innocent of actual literary composition, was the nearest thing to an author in sight.

Having gazed his fill, Mr. Lehman proceeded.

"Now. The next is the orchard scene."

This, as has been said, was where Barmy had opinions to express. He revived like a flower in the rains of spring.

"Ah, yes, the jolly old orchard scene," he said briskly. "I'll tell you about the good old orchard scene. The trees aren't planted right."

Mr. Lehman rose from his seat, and Jack McClure, always one for pouring oil on troubled waters, begged him to take it easy.

"Oh, they aren't, huh?"

"No, laddie. I mean my blossom. In a real orchard——"

A ghastly calm fell upon Mr. Lehman, the sort of calm which falls upon a volcano just before it starts scattering molten lava while thousands flee.

"Now listen! I'm pretty near fed up with you, get me? You been butting in all night long, one fool idea after another, and I had all I can stand."

"But this isn't a fool idea. It's the goods."

"Well, I don't want to hear it, see? Who's producing this show, anyhow?"

"I'm part producer——"

"Yah? Well, I'm the main producer, see? And I'm going to do the talking. Twenty-five per cent, that's what you got."

"Yes, I know, but, dash it, you told me to take notes——"

"You're going to keep on, are you?"

"But, Lord love a duck, if I see that something's wrong, I mean to say, surely I can bung in the word in season? An orchard isn't planted that way. Years ago, when a slip of a boy," said Barmy, becoming reminiscent, "I used to go and spend my summer holidays with an old aunt of mine in the country—to be exact, my Aunt Ysobel at Lower-Smattering-on-the-Wissel in the county of Worcestershire—and she had an orchard and, believe me or believe me not——"

The volcano erupted.

"Sweet suffering soup spoons!" cried Mr. Lehman, clutching at his hat, the only stable thing in a whirling universe. "It's too much. You half wreck the show, prowling around backstage and annoying artists, and then you come here shooting your head off about trees and orchards and your Aunt Agatha."

"Ysobel. Spelled with a Y."

"What in blazes do you know about show business? I'm running this show, see, and I want you to butt out of it, see? I had all I can stand, and I want you to keep out. When bigger half-wits are born, they'll have twice the sense you have. Stop talking and save the wear and tear on your tonsils. Get me?"

Dinty rose from her seat. She was pale, but composed. She had observed Barmy's lower jaw droop like a dying lily, and the sight had aroused all that was maternal in her.

"Don't talk to him like that! I won't stand for it."

Mr. Lehman turned a red eye on this mutineer in the camp.

"Oh? Now it's your business, is it?"

Dinty was a Moore from County Kerry, and you can push County Kerry Moores only so far. Her lips tightened, her eyes glowed. It seemed for a moment as if she was about to handle Mr. Lehman as she had handled the insurance salesman named Ed at Coney Island.

She fought down the impulse.

"Yes, it is. You take his money—all that you could chisel out of him—for a play you must have known hadn't a dog's chance, and every time he opens his mouth, you shout at him. You listen to switchboard girls and waiters, but——"

"Is that so? And who asked you to say anything?"

"I've kept quiet as long as I could."

"Yah? Well, now suppose you try keeping quiet somewheres else. You can get to hell out of here, and you needn't come back."

Barmy spoke. He had been intending to intervene in the debate earlier, but the nobility of Dinty's outburst had stunned him and rendered him incapable of speech.

"Just a minute," said Barmy, realizing too late that the first two words should have been pronounced 'Jussa'. "Not so dam quick, my puss. This jolly old room happens to be *my* jolly old room, and what I mean to say . . . Well, to cut a long story short and get down to the nub, you can't go about the place ordering people out of it."

"I can't, eh?"

"Definitely not. That's official."

"I warn you to lay off me."

"I'm dashed if I'll lay off you."

"Oh? So besides running the show, you're trying to run me? To hell with you. Go on back to London or whatever Limey town it was you said you come from, and take her with you, because she's fired."

Barmy's voice, which had climbed well into the higher register, rose higher.

"Fired, eh?" He laughed a harsh and mocking laugh. "Let me tell you, my old sport, that she wouldn't work for you any longer, anyhow. Do you want to know why?"

"I'd love to."

"Because she's going to work for me, my blossom, that's jolly well why. You think I don't know anything about show business.

I'll show you whether I know anything about show business.
Do you want to sell the rest of it to me. . . the play?"

"Do I *what*?"

"You heard. How about it? Think on your feet, sweetheart."

A certain thoughtfulness had replaced the belligerency of Mr.
Lehman's manner. He looked at Jack McClure, and noting on
that gentleman's face the expression of one who has just become
convinced that there is a Santa Claus, saw his way clear before
him.

"I might," he said slowly. "For a price. It's a valuable property.
What do you say, Jack?"

"Up to you."

"McClure and me is in together. Give us . . . ten thousand
apiece, and the show's yours."

"I'll give you five thousand apiece."

"Seventy-five hundred."

"Five thousand."

"Cash?"

Dinty uttered a wail.

"Barmy, you can't!"

Barmy ignored the interruption. One keeps the women out
of these things.

"Cash," he said. "Ten thousand dollars, cash down, for
Lehman Productions—all of it."

"Set!" said Mr. Lehman.

"Set!" said Jack McClure.

Barmy went to his suitcase. His faithful cheque-book was there.
As he groped for it, it seemed to him to shrink away, as if it were
trying to hide. He wrote the cheque, and handed it with a flourish
to Mr. Lehman, who took it devoutly and said he guessed that
was that. And Jack McClure said he guessed that was that.

"And now," said Barmy, "if you wouldn't all mind leaving——"

The room emptied itself. Only Fanny lingered. Her face wore
a look of gravity, as if she were preparing to do seven clubs
instead of six for the wow at the finish. She hesitated for a
moment, as if about to say something, then seemed to change
her mind.

She shrugged her shoulders, and went out.

★ 17 ★

"O<small>H</small>, Barmy" wailed Dinty. "Why did you do it? Why?"

To Barmy, still breathing fire through his nostrils, the question seemed a foolish one. It was as if a damsel in distress, rescued from a two-headed giant by a knight errant, had called upon the latter to give a brief explanation of his behaviour.

"Why?" he snorted. "What else could I do, dash it, when he started giving you the old raspberry like that? Had to put the blighter in his place, what?"

"But your last ten thousand dollars!"

"Eh?"

"The last ten thousand dollars you had in the world."

Barmy sat down heavily, as if his legs had been mown from under him. The heady exhilaration which comes from making a great gesture had buoyed him up so far, but its aid had suddenly failed him. He felt as though his spine had been withdrawn from his body and a cheap spaghetti substitute inserted in its place.

"I see what you mean," he said. "Yes, you have a point there. Still," he went on, brightening, "I own the play now."

"But how are you going to run it?"

"Eh? Why—I suppose—er—just run it, as it were."

"But what *with*? Oh, Barmy, I hate to be such a crêpe-hanger, but it's no good not facing it. Don't you know what happens to shows on the road before they come into New York? They never make a cent. They always lose money. Thousands of dollars unless you have the most tremendous luck. You'll need at least another ten thousand to cover expenses and keep the thing going."

"I will?"

"Otherwise you'll just have to close and cut your losses."

A delicate green had begun to steal into Barmy's face. He looked like a passenger on a Folkestone to Boulogne boat who has just become sensitive to the vessel's motion.

"This opens up a new line of thought," he said. "You really

mean that? There positively is no hope of navigating under our own steam and paying the weekly bills as we go?"

"None, I'm afraid."

"Then shall I tell you something," said Barmy, becoming greener. "I'm ruined. I'm a spent egg. I'm a . . . What was that thing I used to sing in my bath quite a good deal? Ah, yes. 'I'm a worthless cheque, a total wreck, a flop.' Possibly the wisest course would be to end it all. You don't happen to have a fluid ounce or two of cyanide on you, do you?"

"You mustn't talk like that. We'll get through this somehow. Something will happen, I know. I just feel that something is going to happen."

"So do I. And I wish it wasn't."

The telephone rang shrilly. Barmy took up the receiver with a weary gesture.

"Hullo? . . . Yah, this is Mr. Phipps . . . What do you mean? Of course there isn't . . . Oh, sorry, yes, there is . . . All right. Yes, I see what you mean. Right ho." He hung up and moodily announced the bad news. "That was the office, accusing me—with some show of justice, I admit—of having a member of the gentler sex in my room. You aren't allowed on the premises, apparently. It's against the rules."

"Oh, damn the rules!"

"I couldn't agree with you more wholeheartedly, but I suppose we shall have to humour the sons of bachelors. We don't want a bevy of stern-faced men coming up and leading you out with gyves upon your wrists. You'd better buzz off."

"But we must talk this thing over."

"True. Lots of stones to turn and avenues to explore. I see that."

"How are you going to get some money?"

"Ah! You may well ask. That's the very problem I was turning over in my mind myself."

"Do you think there's anyone in Syracuse with ten thousand dollars?"

"I don't think there's anyone anywhere with ten thousand dollars."

"You told me once you had a rich uncle in England. Couldn't you cable him?"

"And try to bite his ear for the sum needed?"

"Yes."

"Ha!"

"What?"

"I merely said 'Ha!'. Did you ever read *Alice Through The Looking Glass*?"

"Yes, years ago."

"Remember the Jabberwocky?"

"Of course."

"Uncle Theodore. The jaws that bite, the claws that catch! One move on my part to try to separate him from ten thousand of the best and brightest, and he would come whiffling through the tulgey wood and burble as he came. At the moment, I don't mind telling you, I am not high up on the list of his favourite buddies. One of these days I must show you the letter he wrote me on receiving the information that J. G. Anderson had given me the bum's rush. It was a fruity letter, full of good stuff. No, if you had been entertaining any idea of Uncle Theodore as a promising prospect for the quick touch, abandon same. I've about as much chance of tapping him for the needful as I have of strolling into Fort Knox with a spade and bucket and helping myself to contents."

Dinty bit her lip.

"It's a mess, isn't it?"

"A Grade A. mess. But with one bright spot in it, if messes have bright spots. I may be down among the wines and spirits— I will go further. I *am* down among the wines and spirits—but at least I met you."

"If only you hadn't!"

"What do you mean, if only I hadn't? Lord love a duck, it's the one aspect of the whole bally affair that you can't find a flaw in. I may be down to my last bean, I may have to starve in the jolly old gutter, but at any rate I've known you. It makes up for everything. Purified in the holocaust of a mighty love, I shall wander out into the bread line a finer, deeper man. Gosh, how I love you, young Dinty."

"And I love you, Barmy."

Barmy reeled. He stared at her incredulously, and noted that her eyes were shining like, as he put it to himself in a happy flash of inspiration, twin stars.

"You do?"

"Of course I do. I always did, right from the beginning."

"Not when I set your hat on fire?"

"Not then, perhaps, but next day, when you told me you had put that money in the show just so as to be near me. I suddenly realized that you were the most wonderful man in the world."

"Would you go as far as that?"

"There's nobody like you."

"That's what my Uncle Theodore has often observed. Only he didn't say it the way you do. More with a sort of nasty rasp in his voice, if you know what I mean. Dinty, you don't really love me, do you? You're kidding me, aren't you? What they call ribbing over here."

"Of course I'm not kidding you."

Barmy swelled like a balloon.

"Then to hell and blazes," he cried, "with ruin and gutters and bread lines and what not! Nothing else matters but that. If you love me, I laugh at ruin," said Barmy, doing so. "And I'll tell you something," he proceeded, all fire and enthusiasm. "I'll get that money. I'll get it somewhere . . . somehow, if I have to burgle a bank. And the play. It might be a success in New York, don't you think?"

"Well——"

"I mean, I know it isn't frightfully good, but that isn't supposed to matter much in New York, is it? If I can just get that money . . . enough to keep us going——"

He broke off. An unseen hand had knocked on the door.

"Gosh!" he said, suddenly deflated. It had sounded like the hand of doom. He looked at Dinty, and Dinty looked at him. Here, they both were thinking, was that bevy of stern-faced men with the gyves.

"Who's there?" quavered Barmy.

"It's Mr. Fritchie, Mr. Phipps."

"Oh, what ho, Mr. Fritchie. It's the screwball," said Barmy in a hoarse aside. He opened the door. "It wasn't locked," he said defensively.

"I was just leaving," said Dinty.

"Huh?" Mr. Fritchie looked about him. "Oh, broke up early, eh?"

"This is . . . Mr. Fritchie. Miss Moore."

"How are you, Mr. Fritchie?"

"Well, I'll tell you. My throat's not too good——"

Barmy resumed the speech for the defence.

"The door wasn't locked, and Miss Moore was just going out."

"Huh?"

"Isn't that what you came about? Someone just telephoned from the office, beefing about Miss Moore being here."

"Oh, that was only Mr. Hemingway. He's a dope. Don't pay any attention to Mr. Hemingway."

"Well, that's fine," said Barmy, relieved. "Come in and take a chair."

Oscar Fritchie took a chair. He was a stoutish young man with a vacant face and large, myopic eyes. He looked like a sheep with horn-rimmed spectacles. Anyone who had ever seen a sheep wearing horn-rimmed spectacles would have recognized immediately its resemblance to the assistant manager of the Mayflower Hotel, Syracuse. His rather bleating voice increased the illusion.

"How was everything?" he said. "All right? The supper?"

"Oh, terrific, thanks."

"I see you got the champagne."

"Yes, rather."

"I told the waiter to be sure to ice it. Did he?"

"Absolutely. Like billy-o."

Oscar Fritchie explained his policy.

"You see, we get show-troupes right along up here, and I know they got the habit of getting together, sort of, so I kind of make a point of seeing that everything's all right. I'm sorry your party's broken up."

"Yes, too bad."

"I'd have liked to meet them. I've always had a kind of liking for theatrical people," said Oscar Fritchie, starting to converse easily, "and of course they stop here at the hotel a lot, and some of them sort of let me come around."

"I see."

"Ian Keith was here last year. We had quite a long talk. You know how it is," said Oscar Fritchie. "You get a liking for something. The theatre, I mean. All my life I've . . . just kind of liked to talk to theatrical people. I guess maybe it's because I've always had a sort of feeling I might get into the theatre myself some day. Pardon?" said Oscar Fritchie, looking inquiringly at Dinty, who had leaped some inches into the air with a sharp cry.

"Cramp," said Dinty.

"Huh?"

"I got a touch of cramp."

"Is that so? I get a touch of cramp sometimes. Comes on sudden."

"Yes, doesn't it," said Dinty, and gave Barmy the sort of look which in Keats's poem the soldiers of stout Cortez directed at one another when standing silent upon a peak in Darien. It was almost identically the same look which Barmy had shot at her. Here, one would have said, and in saying would have been a hundred per cent correct, were two minds with but a single thought.

Barmy cleared his throat.

"Would you mind repeating that?" he said in a low voice.

"Huh?"

"About the theatre."

"I like it."

"And you think that some day you might get into it yourself?"

"That's what."

There was an awed silence.

"You mean . . . as a producer?" said Dinty.

"As a producer, do you mean?" said Barmy.

"That's what I'd like."

"Sit down!" cried Dinty.

"Sit down!" cried Barmy.

"I am sitting down," said Oscar Fritchie.

"Oh, yes, so you are. Silly of me."

Dinty drew a deep breath.

"Do you own this hotel, Mr. Fritchie?"

"Me? No, I'm the assistant manager. Mr. Hemingway owns it."

"Still, I suppose that's a pretty good position, assistant manager? You must make a lot of money."

"Oh, I don't suppose you folks would call it much."

Barmy, noticing a speck of lint on the visitor's coat sleeve, flicked it off in a loving manner.

"Have you . . ." He paused, searching for the right words. "Have you been able to . . . Have you got any saved up?"

"Huh?"

"Mr. Phipps worked in a hotel, too, before he went into the theatrical business," explained Dinty brightly. "He has known so many hotel men who didn't save. He just hopes you're different."

Oscar Fritchie nodded in a rather superior manner. He was proud of his thrift.

"That's right. A lot of them don't."

"But you do?"

"You bet your life I do. What's the matter?"

"Not a thing. Just another touch of cramp."

"You got it, too?" asked Mr. Fritchie, looking at Barmy.

"The merest twinge. I say, would you care for a stoup of champagne?"

"That's not a bad idea. You know, I like you folks. You make a fellow feel nice."

"Some more?"

"I'm not robbing you?"

"Not a bit."

Oscar Fritchie sipped at his glass.

"Yes, sir," he said, "I always say theatre folks are nice people. Not stuck up . . . You know . . . Make a fellow feel at home. I guess that's why I've always liked it . . . sort of . . . the show business."

"There's no business like show business," said Dinty. "You remember the song?"

"You betcher. I can sing it."

"Go ahead."

"Well, not right now. Some other time."

"Any time that suits you."

Barmy had found another piece of lint, and was busy removing it. His hand being so conveniently placed for the gesture, he patted Oscar Fritchie's arm.

"Er——"

"Huh?"

"Nothing yet," said Barmy, his nerve failing him.

Oscar Fritchie regarded him with a perplexed frown.

"Say, what's up?"

Dinty leaped into the breach. Women are braver than men.

"I know what Mr. Phipps was going to say, Mr. Fritchie. He has a proposition to make to you."

"He has?"

"He's going to give you the chance to invest in this play of his that opened tonight. It's going to make an awful lot of money."

"Millions," said Barmy, himself again now that his path had been made straight. "Millions, my blossom, millions. And you've only to say the word, and you get your slice."

Oscar Fritchie scratched his left eyebrow. The proposal

attracted him, but as so often happens on these occasions, he was conscious of a certain coldness about the feet. It made him waver. If Shakespeare had happened to enter the room at this moment with a friend, he would have said to the friend: 'Don't look now, but that fellow in the horn-rimmed spectacles over there will give you some idea of what I was driving at when I wrote that stuff about letting "I dare not" wait upon "I would", like the poor cat in the adage."

"Oh . . . now . . er——" said Oscar Fritchie.

Dinty pressed him hotly.

"Now wait! Wait! It's a wonderful opportunity, Mr. Fritchie. You didn't see the show tonight, did you?"

"No."

"That's fine. It's going to be much better. There was an understudy playing the leading part tonight."

"And you know what that means," said Barmy. "Before I bring it into New York, I shall get a regular star. Someone big."

"Maurice Evans, perhaps," said Dinty.

"Or the Lunts," said Barmy.

"The Lunts wouldn't be bad," Dinty agreed. "Or Clark Gable."

"Yes, Gable might do," said Barmy.

"Someone big, anyway," said Dinty.

"Yes, someone big," said Barmy.

Dinty had now attached herself to the lapel of Mr. Fritchie's coat, and was twisting it.

"Mr. Phipps will tell you what a wonderful play this is, Mr. Fritchie. It's simply marvellous. And he has bought his partners out and has got hold of the whole thing."

"Lock, stock and barrel," said Barmy.

"Yes, lock, stock and barrel. It's a real chance, the chance of a lifetime."

"It sounds kind of good," admitted Oscar Fritchie. "But on the other hand——"

"What an amazing coincidence," said Barmy, flicking off some more lint. "That's exactly absolutely what I said myself, when I was offered a slice of the thing. I don't mind telling you I hesitated at first, quite a bit. One's got to be careful. But once I'd been told the story——"

"Oh, baby!" said Dinty.

"Precisely," said Barmy. "Oh, baby! I could see it was terrific.

I knew it was going to be a knock-out. There's a priest in it, and
a rabbi, and they come in and gab back and forth, and the feller
shoots the feller, only he doesn't really, it's the brother. And so
on and so on and back and forth and back and forth, and then
off you go to Hong Kong. A great big scene instead of where
it's a cabaret. It's wonderful. It's a hop joint and the priest comes
in, only he's a missionary now, and he wants to close up the
place and the hero comes back at him with the strong talk
and so-and-so, and-so-and-so, and the girl gets more sympathy
because we're writing in a baby. And then they all go to heaven
in the last act and put on wings and there's a fat part for God.
There's absolutely never been anything like it. It's going to
be the biggest thing there ever was in the theatre. So how
about it, my puss?"

Oscar Fritchie, having done all that was possible to his left
eyebrow, had started to scratch the other one. It was plain that
he had been swayed, as who would not have been, by Barmy's
eloquence.

"Go into the theatrical business?" he murmured musingly.
"It would be sort of fun."

"Oh, it's an awful lot of fun," said Dinty. "You haven't any
idea."

"Would it cost much?"

Barmy reassured him.

"Practically nothing. You can have twenty-five per cent of it
for thirty thousand dollars."

"Thirty?"

"Twenty-five."

"Twenty-five?"

"Twenty."

"Twenty?"

"Fifteen. Or, putting it another way, ten."

"But that's the very lowest, Mr. Fritchie," said Dinty, giving
the coat lapel another loving twist.

Oscar Fritchie scratched his chin.

"It's a lot of money."

"No, no. A bargain. Only you've got to decide quick, because
so many people are after it. You see, that's how theatrical business
is. You have to make quick decisions."

"Absolutely," said Barmy. "I mean Yah. The bimbo who
decides right away—standing up—he's the bird who drags home

the gravy. Why, there was a fellow we know who could have bought in on *Arsenic and Harvey*, only he didn't think standing up, so look at him. Didn't get a smell of it. That's show business."

"That's show business," said Dinty.

There was not much more of Oscar Fritchie's exposed portions left to scratch, but he scratched what there was.

"I—I don't know what to say. I been getting kind of tired of the hotel lately——"

"Of course you have," said Dinty sympathetically. "You're not the kind of man to stay cooped up in a hotel all his life. Look at Mr. Phipps."

Oscar Fritchie looked at Mr. Phipps.

"He's got out, and where is he now?"

"Ah!" said Barmy, waving a spacious arm and upsetting the visitor's glass.

Oscar Fritchie found that he had not scratched the tip of his nose. He repaired the omission.

"I'd love to quit and tell Mr. Hemingway what I thought of him."

"That's the spirit!" said Dinty. "Why don't you?"

"I'm scared."

"You won't get another chance like this to leave this old hotel behind you. You'll be sorry if you let it go."

"Yes," said Barmy, thoroughly concurring. "I should imagine that if a man had to look back at a colossal opportunity he'd missed, as it might be this one, it would make him pretty bitter, pretty bitter. He'd brood a bit, I bet."

"He'd be eaten by remorse," said Dinty.

"To the bone," said Barmy.

Oscar Fritchie quivered. No man likes to think that he is going to spend a lifetime of vain regrets, brooding on what might have been.

"It wants thinking about."

"Do it on your feet."

"You say it's a good play?"

"Terrific."

Oscar Fritchie started in again on his left ear. His defences were crumbling.

"There are certainly some things I'd tell Mr. Hemingway, the big stiff," he murmured, like a man communing with his immortal soul.

"Write a receipt," said Barmy.

"Okay, boss."

"Now wait," said Oscar Fritchie. "Wait a moment."

"You can't wait in show business. Unless you can give us your cheque on the spot," said Barmy, "the whole thing's off. Can you?"

"I haven't said I was going to at all, yet."

Dinty smiled her bright smile. That suggestion of the maternal came into her manner. She conveyed the impression that if she had not been busy writing the receipt, she might have patted Oscar Fritchie's head.

"Just think, Mr. Fritchie. If you sign this agreement, you can go to Mr. Hemingway tonight and tell him all those things."

"He's in bed."

"Pull him out of it."

Oscar Fritchie considered this. It was an alluring idea.

"I suppose he makes you work very hard?"

"Twelve hours a day."

"Awful!"

"Monstrous!" said Barmy. "In the theatre you don't have to work at all. It's just fun. We're just one happy family. And look," said Barmy. "There's no reason why we have to produce just this one show. We could go ahead and do a lot more. When this is a big success. Why, we can be the biggest producers there are. All kinds of shows . . . Shall I open this for you?" said Barmy, clutching at the cheque-book which had stolen almost imperceptibly from Oscar Fritchie's pocket.

"No, no. I can do it."

"Well, here's ink and everything, and here's the pen of the gardener's aunt. You make the cheque out to me. Cyril Phipps. C-y-r-i-l."

"What's your first name, Mr. Fritchie?" said Dinty. "And how do you spell this one?"

"Oscar Fritchie. F-r-i-t-c-h-i-e. But I haven't made up my mind yet."

"Here's the receipt," said Dinty. "It says you're giving Mr. Phipps ten thousand dollars for twenty-five per cent of the show. Is that all right?"

"Well . . . say . . ."

"Perfectly all right," said Barmy. "Couldn't be better. Now

all you have to do is to write the good old cheque, and all will be joy and laughter."

"Do you think I ought to?"

"Of course you ought to. It's a great big drama, not highbrow, not lowbrow, just medium-brow, and a feller shoots a feller and the priest and the rabbi gab back and forth and there's an orchard in it and Mr. Hemingway comes in . . . Ah!" said Barmy, grabbing at the cheque.

"Look out," said Oscar Fritchie. "It's wet."

"I'll dry it."

"I wonder if I done the right thing."

"Of course you done the right thing. You've set yourself on the broad highway that leads to wealth and fame and, in a nutshell, what not. It's going to be a whale of a hit, sweetheart, a whale of a hit!"

"That's my old Phipps! That's the Phipps I used to know! You never spoke a truer word, my old friend Phipps."

It was not Oscar Fritchie who said this. The voice was the voice of Mervyn Potter. The errant star was standing in the doorway, supporting himself with a hand on either side.

A great change had taken place in Mervyn Potter since Barmy had last seen him, a change very much for the better. Before, he had been in the depths, a broken man headed for the nearest recruiting station of the French Foreign Legion. Now he seemed quietly happy. His wide, pebble-beach smile betrayed intoxication, but it was a gay light-hearted intoxication. Still stinko, he had become joyously stinko. The vultures which had gnawed at his bosom appeared to have downed tools.

"You bet it's going to be a whale of a hit," he proceeded, recklessly removing his hands from their support and zigzagging to a chair, into which he fell like a sack of coals. "And I'll tell you why. I am going to star in it, Phipps, old friend. Back to the army again, sergeant, back to the army again. Mervyn Potter reporting for duty," said Mervyn Potter, rising, saluting and immediately falling back again into his seat, like another sack of coals.

"What!" cried Barmy.

Mervyn Potter, who had closed his eyes as if about to drop into one of his refreshing sleeps, opened them.

"Phipps," he said, "when we had that last stimulating little chat of ours, I think—correct me if I am wrong—I told you that my fiancée—Heloise, only daughter of C. Hamilton Brimble of King's Point, Long Island, assisted by Mrs. C. Hamilton Brimble of King's Point, Long Island—had given me the brusheroo."

"That's right."

"I fancy—again correct me if I am wrong—that I mentioned that my heart was broken."

"That's right."

"Mended," said Mervyn Potter, patting the left side of his waistcoat. "Sound as a bell. Not a crack in it. Mervyn Potter is himself again."

"That's good."

"Not good," corrected Mervyn Potter. "Colossal. Yes," he proceeded, "for a time Heloise's heartless inhumanity upset me quite a little. The sun seemed darkened. Life appeared to be at an end. But mark the sequel. I stepped around to an excellent bar at no great distance from this hotel, and there shot perhaps half a dozen quick ones down the hatch. I then subjected the whole affair to a close review, analysing every facet of it. And all of a sudden a remarkable change came over my mood. I perked up and saw that all had been for the best and that, so far from wallowing in the soup, I had been saved from the scaffold at the eleventh hour, precisely like those fellows in the historical novels, who, as the hangman is adjusting the noose, perceive a horseman riding up on a foaming horse, waving a paper."

He sat for a while musing.

"This whole business of getting married, Phipps," he resumed, "is a thing you have to look at from every angle. What suddenly struck me like a blow was the reflection that a girl like Heloise Brimble would have insisted on a fashionable wedding with full choral effects. There would have been a Bishop, possibly two Bishops, and assistant clergy and bridesmaids and choir boys and reporters and photographers and about eleven hundred guests of assorted sexes. And as I tottered up the aisle, these Bishops, these assistant clergy, these bridesmaids, these reporters, these photographers and these guests would have laughed their fat heads off at me, making me feel like a piece of cheese. Add vergers, sextons, beadles, pew-openers, first and second gravediggers and what not, and take into consideration the fact that after the ceremony would have come the reception at the home of the bride, and can you wonder that I felt that I had had a merciful escape? I tottered from that bar, Phipps, ashen to the lips but with my heart singing within me. I realized that the guardian angel of the Potters, instead of being, as I had supposed, asleep at the switch, had in reality been working like a beaver in my interests, saving me from an experience so terrible as to make the imagination boggle. And as I walked along the street, I met a baby."

Mervyn Potter paused, and a strong shudder shook him.

"I don't know," he went on, his voice trembling, "if all babies in Syracuse are like that, or whether this one was sent especially to warn me. It was one of those bulging babies. It looked a little like Boris Karloff and a little like Winston Churchill. Our eyes met, and it was as though a voice from above had whispered in my ear, 'See, Potter! But for excellent staff work on the part of your guardian angel, something like that might have happened to you!' You may say that a thing like that would not have happened to me, but how do you know? Better men than I have produced babies of an even greater repulsiveness. Some of my best friends are the fathers of the world's leading gargoyles, and who shall say that I would have escaped unscathed? At any rate, be that as it may, my last doubts as to the wisdom of Providence in foiling my matrimonial plans were removed. A heavy burden seemed to fall from my shoulders. I inflated my chest. I gloried in my youth. I abandoned all idea of joining the Foreign Legion and decided to come back to you and resume my place in the troupe. So here I am, Phipps, up and doing with a heart for any fate. Standing shoulder to shoulder like, as I believe I once mentioned to you before, the Boys of the Old Brigade, we will take this play into New York and knock their ruddy eyes out. I've had a great idea. Do you know what we are going to do, Phipps, old friend? We are going to play this charade for laughs. We're going to kid the pants off it and have the customers rolling in the aisles. This opus is not a drama, it's a farce. And when you reflect that if I had remained on the wagon, I should never have thought of that, it makes you realize what a great big wonderful world it is, does it not? Is that a bottle which I see before me, its handle toward my hand?" asked Mervyn Potter, interested. "Or is it but a bottle of the mind, a false creation proceeding from the heat-oppressed brain?"

"Eh? Oh, yes. One bot as per memo. Champagne."

"Come let me clutch thee," said Mervyn Potter.

A stunned silence, the silence of happiness too deep for speech, had fallen on Room 726.

It was broken by Oscar Fritchie.

"Say, could I have your autograph, Mr. Potter?" said Oscar Fritchie.

INASMUCH as the compact little drama *Sacrifice* had opened in Syracuse toward the end of September and had then gone on to play Albany, Worcester and Providence, it was not until nearly the end of October that it completed its preliminary tour and had what in motion picture circles is known as its preemeer on Broadway. To be exact, October the twenty-seventh.

As Dinty Moore entered the office of Lehmac Productions on the morning of October the twenty-eighth, she had a sudden illusion that joy bells were ringing through the world. It was, however, only the telephone, and she hastened to answer it.

"Lehmac Productions," she said in her official voice, the one with the rising lilt. "Noo, Mr. Phipps has not come in yet. Yace, it looks like a very big hit does it not? . . . Oo, well I don't knoo. I believe Mr. Phipps was thinking of producing it himself in London. Maybe if you give him a ring later. *Good*-baye," said Dinty and, hanging up, executed a few dance steps across the floor.

The success of *Sacrifice* had probably not come as a surprise to whoever it was who had been speaking at the other end of the wire, for there are no surprises in the theatre today. Thirty years ago it was possible for a play to steal quietly out into the hinterland and arrive in New York still an unknown quantity, but nowadays *Variety* has its spies everywhere, and the chances of even the most modest enterprise are weighed week by week. The fierce light that beats upon a throne is a mere glimmer compared to that which beats upon a new theatrical production.

To any knowledgeable citizen of Broadway such headlines as:

SACRIFICE NEAT $15,000 ALBANY

SACRIFICE SOLID WOW WORCESTER

and, above all,

SACK SWEET SOCKO 20 G. PROVIDENCE

had told the story. The word had gone around that—unless, of course, these out-of-town triumphs failed to repeat themselves under the more testing conditions of the metropolis—Sack was in. And so it had proved. Unquestionably, indubitably, uncontrovertibly and past all dispute, as Mr. Roget would have put it in his *Thesaurus*, it was a sweet socko.

Time marched on. There were further telephone conversations. Two callers arrived, asking to see Mr. Phipps, and Dinty promised that their visits should be drawn to the attention of the man up top, if and when he put in an appearance. And eventually Barmy came in, on his face the awed look of one who has seen visions.

"What ho, queen of my soul," he said in a hushed voice.

"Pip-pip, maestro," said Dinty, returning civility for civility.

"I say," said Barmy, "did you come here past the theatre?"

"I did."

"Was there really a line of people at the box office?"

"There was, my poppet. A long line. And they all had their four-eighty clutched in their hot little hands, bless them."

Barmy drew a deep breath. If Dinty, too, had observed the spectacle, it could be accepted as official.

"I could hardly believe it. I thought I saw them, but I couldn't help feeling that it was just a beautiful dream. Didn't you think they looked extraordinarily attractive?"

"Fine fellows."

"The salt of the earth. I don't know where you can find more splendid specimens of humanity than in the line waiting at the box office of a show you've bunged a lot of money into. Talk about fair women and brave men! Oh, Dinty!"

Barmy seemed to expand, as if a load had been removed from his shoulders. There had been times during the past four weeks when doubts had assailed him and melancholy had marked him for its own, principally on the occasions when his partner, Mr. Fritchie, had been suffering from one of those attacks of cold feet which were so frequent with him. Moody, wavering, irresolute, Oscar Fritchie was the sort of man who would have got on well with Hamlet. He seemed to find it impossible to look on the bright side. Tell Oscar Fritchie that the house was all sold out for tonight, and he would reply 'But who'll come tomorrow night?', and this kind of thing cannot but have a lowering effect on the most ebullient.

But now that a Broadway first night audience had received the

show rapturously, now that eight critics out of nine had sub-
mitted excellent notices (and the ninth not too dashed bad), now
that long queues of charming and intelligent playgoers were
lining up at the box office, eager to shower their money on the
autocrat behind the window, Barmy had blossomed like some
lovely flower. His eyes gleamed. His butter-coloured hair seemed
to shine. He held himself jauntily and gave the impression of
being three inches taller than he actually was. It was with the air
of a conquering knight coming home to his lady after a successful
couple of years at the Crusades that he now folded Dinty in a
close embrace, covered her upturned face with burning kisses
and told her that of all the outstanding eggs that ever drew
perfumed breath, she was the most pre-eminent.

"I love you, young Dinty."

"Not so much as I love you."

"Much more than you love me."

"You couldn't. Still, let's not quarrel about it. Isn't it wonderful, Barmy, that all this happened? Do you realize that we shall
be rich?"

"Rolling."

"We'll live on Park Avenue."

"With a butler."

"Two butlers. And we'll get a really good car."

"Several really good cars. How about a yacht?"

"I wonder if we could buy the *Queen Mary?*"

"We'll have a jolly good try. And now, touching on this business
of converting you into Mrs. C. Fotheringay-Phipps, what's the
procedure? Give me the lowdown straight from the horse's
mouth. I say," said Barmy, in sudden alarm, "you don't want a
fashionable wedding with full choral effects, do you? And that
stuff Potter was talking about . . . the Bishop and assistant clergy
and bridesmaids and choir boys and sextons and beadles and
first and second gravediggers and all that?"

"Of course not. I want to be married in the Little Church
Around The Corner."

"Where's that?"

"Twenty-ninth Street."

"Quiet sort of place?"

"We shall have it all to ourselves."

"Except for the parson."

"I don't see how you could keep him out."

"No, admit the parson. And possibly a brace of witnesses?"

"I suppose so."

"But that's the lot?"

"That's the lot."

"Then ho for the Little Church Around The Corner. Come on, grab your hat and let's go."

Dinty regarded him maternally.

"My poor child, you can't rush things like that. You've got to get a licence."

"Couldn't we dispense with all that sort of thing?"

"I'm afraid not. If you blew in without a licence, the minister would throw you out on your ear. And, anyway, you've work to do."

"Work? At a time like this?"

"This is just the moment. All sorts of people have been telephoning and calling. You'll have to spend the rest of the day thinking on your feet and making quick decisions."

"Perhaps you're right," said Barmy. "Yes, I suppose there is man's work to do."

He seated himself in the swivel chair, tilted it back, put his feet on the desk, reached for his hat and placed it on his head.

"Now!" he said. "Tell me all, my puss, omitting no detail, however slight, for one never knows how important the most seemingly trivial detail may be. What's been happening?"

Dinty consulted her notebook.

"There have been two or three telephone calls. One was from someone who wanted to buy the play for London. I told him you were probably going to do it in London yourself."

"Of course I am. And in Paris and Berlin and Moscow."

"You can't do it in Moscow."

"Well, Brussels, then. Where the sprouts come from. Brussels is just as good. Proceed," said Barmy, putting the tips of his fingers together.

"There were two callers. One of them wouldn't leave his name. He was rather mysterious, and said he would be back."

"Did he state his business?"

"No."

Barmy frowned. Laxity here. It would be necessary, he saw, to ginger up the office staff.

"Always ask them to state their business," he said, rebukingly. "And bring their cards in first, to see if I'll see them."

"Yes, sir. I will, sir. Thank you for telling me, sir."

Barmy blushed.

"Was I putting on dog?"

"You were."

"I'm sorry. I keep trying not to, but the fact of the matter is, this thing has given me the most frightful swelled head. I find myself chucking my chest out and jostling people off the sidewalk and being in two minds whether or not to pop round to Lee Shubert's office and call him Lee. Deflate me from time to time, will you? If you see it coming on, just say 'Hoy!' "

"I will."

"Hoy! Sharply, like that."

"Okay, professor."

Barmy mused.

"And yet, dash it all," he said, feeling cheated of his dues, "why shouldn't one stick on a bit of the haughty seigneur and swank around somewhat after a hit like this one? Did you read the notices?"

"I know them by heart. They were wonderful."

"*The Times?*" said Barmy dubiously.

"It wasn't bad?"

"Not bad, no, but . . . I didn't like that bit about the brothel being merely adequate." A stern look came into Barmy's face. "I don't think I'll let *The Times* critic come to my next one. Teach him a sharp lesson."

"Hoy!"

"Hoy it is. Notice how it comes on me in a flash, like a stroke or something? I'll be buzzing along quite all right, and suddenly—*bingo!*—the old head swells up like a poisoned pup. I'll have to see a doctor. Who was the other bird?"

"Which other bird?"

"The other bird who presented himself *chez* Phipps. You said there were two of them."

"Oh, yes. It was your former boss, Mr. Anderson."

Barmy stared.

"J. G. Anderson? Are you sure?"

"I've only his word for it, but that's who he said he was."

"Well, I'll be dashed."

"He said he wanted to see you about something important."

"He did, eh? Then do you know what must have happened? He must have come up to New York on a toot and gone to the show last night and read the papers this morning and seen that I've got a whale of a hit, and he's going to have another try to get me to buy that hotel of his. In Bessemer, Ohio. A fat chance!"

"Why? Why don't you buy the hotel?"

Barmy laughed derisively. The idea amused him.

"Me? What do I want with hotels? If Lee drops in and suggests my taking over half a dozen of his theatres, that's another matter. But hotels!"

"Hoy!"

"Not a bit of it. Hoys don't enter into the thing at all. How could I run a hotel in Ohio when I'm in the legit?"

"Get out of the legit."

Barmy gaped. He could hardly believe that he had heard her aright.

"What, chuck show business just when I'm sitting on top of the world?"

"But it's so precarious, my pet. You're up today and down tomorrow. *Sacrifice* is a hit but your next one might be a terrible flop. And the next one after that, and the next one after that. A hotel's different. It's solid. I'd love to help you run a hotel, and I know I'd be happy in a place like Bessemer. I'm sick of Broadway."

Again Barmy found himself doubting his ears.

"Sick of Broadway?"

"Sick to death. Oh, Barmy— "

She broke off. The door had opened, and Oscar Fritchie was coming in.

Externally, Oscar Fritchie looked about the same as he had always done, which was not much, but with his opening words it became evident that internally he was a mere mass of quivering ganglions.

"Say, what are all those people doing over at the theatre?" he asked anxiously, not even waiting to say Good morning. "I come by the theatre just now, and there was a whole bunch of them milling around the lobby."

Barmy tilted his hat and uttered a short laugh. These novices!

"They're buying tickets."

"Tickets?"

"Yah."

"For the show, you mean? Why?"

"It's a big success."

"Who says so?"

"Everybody says so. Didn't you read the notices?"

"What notices?"

"Of the play. In the papers."

"I hadn't the nerve to look at the papers."

"Dinty, have you got the papers?"

"Not here. Shall I go out and buy them?"

"Do so, and with all speed."

"I will, " said Dinty. "And later on, if you have a moment, Mr. Shubert, I'd like to go on with what I was saying when we were interrupted. I have much to say to you on a certain subject."

Oscar Fritchie waited anxiously while the door closed. Then he turned to Barmy and spoke in a hoarse whisper.

"Now, on the level, how are things?"

"It's one of the biggest hits ever produced."

"No, no," said Oscar Fritchie. "She's gone. You can tell me."

"Mobs of eager men are calling up wanting to buy it for London and everywhere."

Oscar Fritchie started.

"How much did you get?"

"I didn't sell it."

"What!"

"Of course I didn't. Sell it, foolish! What the dickens would I want to sell it for?"

Oscar Fritchie clutched piteously at his partner's coat sleeve. His manner was agitated. He bleated like the sheep he so closely resembled.

"Now look. I think if we can get any money, we ought to, huh? . . . because . . . I don't feel just right yet, see?"

Barmy's jolly laugh ridiculed his fears.

"When we go ahead and produce a few more, you'll feel all right."

"Do you think we ought to do that?"

"Of course I do. This is not an end, but a beginning. I'm planning to do a big musical, to start with, with ten comics and a hundred lovely girls."

Oscar Fritchie reached for his hat.

"I think maybe I ought to get out."

"Out of the firm? Right ho. I can handle it myself."

"Would you buy my share?"

"Like a shot."

"Oh?" said Oscar Fritchie, putting his hat down. "Well . . . then . . . I don't know," and you could see Hamlet patting him on the back and telling him he knew just how he felt.

"Do you know what I'm going to do, my blossom?" said Barmy, tilting his hat. "I'm going to get hold of all the big playwrights there are in this country and put them under contract, and then I'm going to buy up all the foreign plays. Make what they call a corner."

Oscar Fritchie's adam's apple was leaping up and down.

"You are?"

"And when I've got all the plays tied up, I'm going to get the theatres."

"The theatres?"

"Yah."

"Buy up a whole lot of theatres?"

"Got to have somewhere to put the plays, what?"

Oscar Fritchie's adam's apple did another quick exercise gallop.

"But look. Suppose something happens? Suppose something goes wrong some place?"

"How can it?"

"It might."

"Not a chance. Shall I tell you the secret of show business? Just give the public what they want."

"But how do you know what they want?"

"They always want the same thing."

"Sure as I went into it," said Oscar Fritchie, shaking his head lugubriously, "they'd change their minds."

Dinty appeared with the papers under her arm and a card in her hand.

"Hoy!" she said, speaking immediately from the doorway.

Barmy eyed her with a touch of guilt.

"Why the Hoy?"

"I'll bet it was needed while I was out of the room."

This was so true that Barmy hastened to change the subject.

"I see you have a card on your person," he said, rather distantly. "Does someone wait without?"

"He does."

Barmy waved a managerial hand at Oscar.

"You see? Not a moment passes but some eager beaver comes muscling in, wanting to do business. Who is he?"

"He's one of the two birds."

"Two birds? Ah, yes. The two birds who called, you mean."

"That's right. This is the first bird. The one who wouldn't leave his name and said he would be back."

"I don't know why," said Oscar Fritchie, beginning to show the early symptoms of palsy, "but I've got a feeling that this is bad news."

Barmy glanced at the card. It held no message for him.

"The bimbo under advisement is a complete and absolute stranger to me. Man and boy, I've knocked about the world quite a bit in my time, but I've never heard of J. Bromley Lippincott."

"Attorney-at-law," said Oscar Fritchie, looking over his shoulder. "That's the part I don't like, that attorney-at-law."

"Did he say what he wanted?"

"Not a word. The silent tomb."

"He must have come to make an offer."

Oscar Fritchie shook his head.

"Not an attorney-at-law. They don't make offers. It wouldn't be something you did before this, maybe, huh?" he said hopefully.

Barmy became the brisk executive.

"Well, I can give him five minutes and hear what he's got to say. Bung him in, young heart's delight."

"Yes, my king."

Oscar Fritchie was now trembling like a leaf.

"You know what?" he said. "I'll bet we've got the show in the wrong theatre."

Before Barmy could comment on this unpleasant thought, Dinty returned, escorting the visitor. And the moment Barmy set eyes on him, he saw that this was a visitor of no common order.

One of those visitors who mark epochs.

★ 19 ★

J. BROMLEY LIPPINCOTT was a tall, dark cadaverous man who
looked about sixty, as he had probably looked at the age of ten,
and gave the impression, not unusual with attorneys-at-law, of
having seen so much of life's murky side that he now automatically
suspected everyone he met of nameless crimes. Formidable was
the word for J. Bromley and sinister the word for the bulging
briefcase which he bore with him like a warrior's shield. Too
small to contain a corpse, except possibly that of a Singer midget,
it was large enough to hold the guilty secrets of half the population
of New York, and the nervous beholder, eyeing it, had visions
of documents suddenly popping out of its interior which would
prove him, the nervous beholder, to be legally debarred from
being a feoffee of any fee, fiduciary or in fee simple or something
of that nature. It was that sort of briefcase.

He laid it on the desk with the air of an executive of the Black
Hand checking a bomb at a restaurant cloakroom, and for a
moment stood facing Barmy and Oscar, allowing his gaze to bore
deep into their sensitive persons. Like the Ancient Mariner, he
held them with a glittering eye.

"Good morning," he said.

Simple words, but he uttered them so much in the manner of a
detective unmasking the murderer in the final chapter of a mystery
thriller that Oscar Fritchie, who had been staring at him with
wide, horrified eyes, started convulsively, as if he had been
lolling in an electric chair and some practical joker had turned
on the juice. It was plain that Oscar Fritchie feared the worst.

Nor was Barmy feeling as nonchalant and lighthearted as he
could have wished to be. There was an indefinable something
about this attorney-at-law which chilled the spirits. Scattered
throughout the United States of America there were probably
men, friends of his boyhood days or old cronies who had gone
through law school with him, who looked on J. Bromley Lippincott as one of the gang and got a pleasurable kick out of his

150

society, but Barmy was not of their number. He was definitely allergic to Mr. Lippincott. Meeting Mr. Lippincott's pale grey eye, he found himself understanding what the Gypsy Sybil had meant when she had spoken of trouble coming from a dark man.

"Did you want to see me?" he said, plucking at his tie, and J. Bromley Lippincott gave him a quick, short, sharp, unplesant look.

"Which is Mr. Cyril Phipps?" he asked in a voice of steel.

"He is," said Oscar Fritchie with vast relief. It was the first suggestion he had had that the blue bird might be among those present.

His relief was short-lived.

"Is this Mr. Oscar Fritchie?" asked the visitor keenly.

The jig was up.

"Yep," said Oscar, commending his soul to God. Nothing could save him now.

"Ah," said Mr. Lippincott, and was silent for a space, his thoughts probably busy with replevin or something of that sort. Then his eye fell on the briefcase and, recalled by the sight of it to the fact that he was here on a mission, he resumed, still speaking in that steely voice which reminded Barmy of his bank manager in London regretting that in the circumstances it would be inconvenient—nay, impossible—to oblige him with the suggested overdraft.

"I called on you gentlemen earlier and left word that I would return."

"Yah? I wish I'd known," said Oscar.

"You have my card?"

Concealment was useless. Barmy confessed to having his card.

"My name is Lippincott."

"That's right. J. Bromley, what?"

"Of Lippincott, Lippincott, Cohn, Mandelbaum and Lippincott."

"A lawyer, huh?"

This was Oscar Fritchie, breezily endeavouring to establish friendly relations. Try for a chummy atmosphere right at the outset, that was the policy of Oscar Fritchie.

"An attorney-at-law," corrected Mr. Lippincott with cold severity. "May I——?" he said, indicating with a gesture that he wished to use the desk.

"Oh, rather," said Barmy, suppressing a desire to rush from

the room and escape to Nova Scotia, and with a hideous, menacing slowness Mr. Lippincott went to the desk and took up the brief-case, holding it lovingly in his hands like a mother dandling her first-born. He opened it and extracted from it a bundle of docu-ments. He put the bundle on the desk, at the same time shooting a keen glance at Barmy and Oscar. He took out a second bundle and placed it beside the first, giving Barmy and Oscar another glance. A third bundle, a third glance, and the preliminaries were completed. He removed his glasses, produced a second pair, adjusted them on his nose, cleared his throat, took up one of the documents and unfolded it. A ray of sunshine peeped in at the window, and he inspected it coldly for a moment, as if warning it to be up to no tricks with *him*.

"Now, gentlemen," he said, and it was evident that he was about to get down to the *res*.

He gave the briefcase an affectionate tap, for he loved the little thing, and cleared his throat again.

"You are the owners," he began, "of Lehmac Productions Incorporated, of Fourteen Hundred and Sixty-Eight Broadway, New York, New York." He paused for a moment, then, as if the words constituted deadly evidence which would strip the mask from their faces once and for all, added in a rasping whisper, "A New York corporation."

Oscar Fritchie, vaguely recollecting films he had seen at Syracuse picture palaces, raised his right hand solemnly.

"We are. But he owns most of it," he said, still hoping for the best.

Mr. Lippincott had not shot his bolt. There was more to come.

"Said corporation being the producers of a dramatic com-position—or play—entitled *Sacrifice*."

"Yah," said Barmy, fogged, but helping the thing along. "It opened last night. At the Broadhurst."

Mr. Lippincott cleared his throat again. From the briefcase, out of which Barmy felt that practically anything could emerge now, he took a magazine with a brightly coloured picture on the cover showing a gentleman in a black mask and correct evening dress insinuating a knife into a lady with nothing much on but step-ins and blood.

"In November, Ninteeen Hundred and Forty-Seven," he resumed, "there appeared in this magazine, *Peppy Tales*, published in New York City, New York, an article of fiction—or novelette—entitled *A Man's Honor*. Said article of fiction having been written by my client, Mr. Rodney Rich, of Worcester, Massachusetts."

He paused again. A deadly pause, like that of a cobra preparing to strike.

"And, as we shall duly prove in court——"

Oscar Fritchie leaped.

"Court?"

"Court."

"I thought you said court," said Oscar Fritchie.

Mr. Lippincott resumed his tale to a flatteringly attentive audience. The minstrel was infirm and old, but he was putting his stuff across.

"And, as we shall duly prove in court, the said novelette was made the basis of a dramatic composition—or play—by one Harley Thompson, since deceased."

"Dead," explained Barmy for Oscar Fritchie's benefit. He had been acquainted with Oscar Fritchie long enough to know that anything over one syllable bothered him.

"Subsequently, as we shall prove, the said play was purchased or acquired by one Joseph Lehman, trading—in association with one John McClure—as Lehmac Productions Incorporated of Fourteen Hundred and Sixty-Eight Broadway, New York, New York, a New York corporation, and by him duly produced."

Mr. Lippincott paused again. The sternness of his manner had become tempered by a touch of sadness. It was as though he were telling himself that he was pretty tough, by golly, prepared for anything and not easily shocked, but that he had now come up against something so revolting, so sickening to anyone who, like himself, believed in Man's kinship with the divine, that he could hardly find words with which to continue. Confront him with double burgage, he seemed to be saying to himself, and he could accept it. He might not like it, but he could make allowances for erring human nature and accept it. And the same thing applied to heirs taken in socage.

But this! My God!

With a strong effort he fought down his feelings, and forced himself to the nauseous task.

"It will be shown," he said, pausing for an instant and eyeing the briefcase as if debating the possibility of a rabbit coming out of it, "that the said dramatic composition—or play—is similar to the aforesaid novelette at one hundred and forty-six points."

Barmy sprang toward the ceiling. An adagio dancer could not have got off the mark more nimbly.

"One hundred and forty-SIX?"

"One hundred and forty-six. And that no fewer than seven characters in the aforesaid play bear the same names as those in the aforesaid novelette."

"Oh, my sainted aunt! But listen——"

"One moment, please." Mr. Lippincott had overcome that touch of sadness. He was now all steel and menace once more. "My client, Mr. Rodney Rich, has received no payment for this play, nor has his permission been sought in any way. It is, in short, a clear case of plagiarism, and one of the most flagrant that it has ever been my privilege to encounter," said Mr. Lippincott, and stopped abruptly, as though, yielding to the influence of the surroundings in which he found himself, he had been about to say, 'It's a whale of a case of plagiarism, sweetheart, a whale of a case of plagiarism!'

Barmy looked at Oscar. Oscar looked at Barmy. Neither seemed to derive any great pleasure or solace from what he saw.

"But . . . But . . . But . . ." said Oscar.

"But listen, my dear old minion of the Law," said Barmy. "We didn't know anything about it, dash it all. I bought it from Mr. Lehman, I mean to say, and then Mr. Fritchie here chipped in and took a slice. We never dreamed there was dirty work at the crossroads."

"Possibly not. I acquit you of any deliberate malice afore-thought. Unfortunately——"

"That's a bad word," said Oscar, wincing.

"Unfortunately my client cannot take that into account. His composition has been produced in dramatic form without his permission. Not unnaturally, he seeks redress."

"Seeks what?" said Oscar.

"Money," said Barmy.

Mr. Lippincott, who now seemed to have abandoned all hope of a rabbit coming out of the briefcase, replaced the documents bundle by bundle and snapped the catch. In the stillness its click sounded like one of those explosions which slay six.

"My purpose in laying these facts before you gentlemen, prior to bringing suit, is to afford you the opportunity, if you so desire, of adjusting the matter outside of court."

"Settle it, you mean?"

"Precisely. Here is the proposition I am authorized to lay before you. My client will accept sixty-six and two-thirds per centum of all profits derived from said play, when, if and as produced, and in those circumstances will permit the play to continue. Failing to receive sixty-six and two-thirds per centum——"

"That's money, too," said Oscar, whose brain was working well this morning. Well, that is to say, for Oscar Fritchie.

"——he will apply for an injunction and cause the play to be closed at once."

Barmy uttered a sharp, agonized cry.

"He'll close it?"

"He will close it."

"Close it?" said Oscar.

"Close it," said J. Bromley Lippincott.

A loud gulping noise broke the impressive silence which followed his words. It proceeded from Oscar Fritchie. He had started to totter toward the door, his horn-rimmed spectacles registering anguish and despair. He was a child in theatrical matters, but he knew enough about conditions in the world of the drama to be aware that if you put money into a play and some-one comes along and closes it, you cannot hope for substantial returns on your investment.

An abstemious man as a rule, he was conscious of an imperious desire for a drink, and a strong one, at that, and he intended to have it immediately.

"Look," he said, addressing Barmy in a low, hollow voice. "Most of it's yours, see? I don't know much about lawyers. You do something and I'll go over and see if the theatre's burned down."

He passed from the room, and silence fell again upon the office of Lehmac Productions Incorporated of Fourteen Hundred and Sixty-Eight Broadway, New York, New York, a New York corporation. Barmy was robbed of speech, and Mr. Lippincott, his task completed, was now preparing to relax, like an executioner in some Oriental court taking a breather after strangling a few odalisques with his bowstring. He opened the briefcase, once more paused as if giving the rabbit a last chance, then put a hand in and produced a bar of nut chocolate, which he proceeded to nibble, explaining that he had had a light breakfast.

Barmy turned to Dinty. All this while she had been standing

by the water-cooler, a silent spectator of the tragedy unfolding itself before her horrified eyes. He felt that if anything constructive was to be accomplished, she must be the one to point the way.

"What do you think we ought to do, Dinty?"

Dinty came forward. Her face was pale and her eyes round. She looked at J. Bromley Lippincott as if trying to detect in his granite features some evidence of human feeling. But Mr. Lippincott, though he seemed to be enjoying the nut chocolate, remained the same impregnable figure of doom whose mere glance, before he had even begun to speak, had taken the sunlight out of this sunny morning.

"Must Mr. Phipps give an answer immediately?"

J. Bromley Lippincott finished the nut chocolate and wiped his fingers daintily on his handkerchief.

"I regret that he must."

"But dash it, I haven't had time——"

"Can't we even talk it over?" asked Dinty.

Mr. Lippincott removed his reading-glasses, took out the pair which he used for distance, wiped them, placed them in position and examined Dinty carefully, as if she had been a knotty point of law.

"This young lady is your adviser?"

"Yah."

"H'm," said Mr. Lippincott. He subjected Dinty to another scrutiny. Possibly something about her reminded him of his mother when a girl. Possibly her appearance recalled some home town belle of his youth whose memory he had laid aside in lavender. At any rate, he softened. That is to say, instead of looking like a First Murderer, he looked like a rather kindlier Second Murderer. "At best," he said, "I could allow but a brief time."

"Well, that's better than nothing."

"Shall we say half an hour?"

"Shall we?" said Barmy.

"Yes," said Dinty.

"Very well. I shall return for your decision in half an hour or," said Mr. Lippincott, making it clear to the meanest intelligence, "thirty minutes."

He picked up the briefcase, licked a morsel of chocolate from the corner of his mouth, and withdrew.

★ 20 ★

IN spite of the fact that a room without J. Bromley Lippincott in it was unquestionably a much jollier place to be in than a room full to overflowing with J. Bromley Lippincott, there was nothing in Barmy's demeanour, as the door closed behind the attorney-at-law, to suggest that he had experienced anything in the nature of a sudden burst of high spirits. In Mr. Lippincott's presence, notably during the concluding stages of the interview, he had looked like a corpse which has been several days in the water, and it was such a corpse that he still resembled. Falling into the routine of his predecessors in this office when things were not going quite as planned, he walked sombrely to the water-cooler and filled himself a paper cup. Only when he had drained this, rather in the manner of Socrates drinking the bowl of hemlock, did he speak.

"We won't buy the *Queen Mary*," he said.

"Oh, Barmy!"

"And one more word. We won't live on Park Avenue. We won't have those cars. And those two butlers of whom we spoke will have to pull up their socks and look around for other situations. Yes, I know," he said moodily, as Dinty flung her arms about his neck and kissed him. "Awfully sweet of you, old bean, and delicate attention much appreciated, but, getting remorselessly down to the nub, no amount of kissing and womanly sympathy can alter the salient fact that I am in the soup and sinking for the third time. And just when everything looked so juicy, dammit."

"You mustn't get discouraged."

Barmy eyed her wanly.

"Did you say 'get'? Was the word you employed 'get'?"

"He may be wrong."

"Those fellows are never wrong."

"You didn't make him show you his proofs."

Barmy shuddered.

"I couldn't bear to look at them. No, he's got the thing all

157

taped out. If he states that the said dramatic composition—or play—is similar to the aforesaid novelette at one hundred and forty-six points, you can put your shirt on it that one hundred and forty-six points is the precise total at which it is similar, and that his client, Mr. Rodney Rich of Worcester, Massachusetts, is going to scoop in sixty-six and two-thirds per centum of all profits derived from said play, precisely as indicated. Sixty-six and two-thirds per centum! And I was going to do such big things."

"You still will."

Barmy shook his head. Oscar Fritchie himself could not have been more despondent.

"Not a chance. I see now that I'm not the sort of bird who does. There are birds who do big things and birds who, in sharp contradistinction, don't. I'm one of the birds who don't. The brain power isn't there. There is a shortage of little grey cells. I remember my Uncle Theodore—it was on the occasion when I broke his meerschaum pipe while endeavouring to do the home a bit of good by swatting a fly which was chucking its weight about in the library—saying that I had as much sense as a village idiot. He was a trifle stirred at the moment, for he loved that pipe passionately and used to spend hours a day colouring it, and it seemed to me that he was letting generous wrath run away with his cool judgment, but I now realize that he was quite right. In fact, he was giving me the breaks. I'm no good. I'm hopeless. I'm just poor old Barmy, the village idiot."

"I love village idiots."

Barmy stared.

"Don't tell me you're still toying with the idea of marrying me?"

"Get that licence, and watch my smoke!"

Into the depths which covered Barmy, black as the pit from pole to pole, there crept a faint ray of sunshine. He did not smile, for much would have to happen before he smiled again, but his V-shaped depression perceptibly lightened. He kissed Dinty with something approaching animation.

Then despondency returned. He released her with a heavy sigh.

"You don't know what you're letting yourself in for. A nice breadwinner I should be under present financial conditions. I doubt if I could win a single slice, let alone support you in the style to which you have been accustomed?"

"A one-room flat in Astoria."

"My resources won't even run to a one-room flat."

"You can get a job."

"I doubt it. We Phippses are not easy to place."

"You had a job before."

"True. I held a portfolio as desk clerk under J. G. Anderson. But I got the post not by merit but through influence. My Uncle Theodore, who breeds Siamese cats, happened to be in New York, paying his annual visit to my late grandfather, and learning that Siamese cat breeders were collecting in gangs at Bessemer, Ohio, decided to join the party. He put up at J. G. Anderson's hotel, met J. G. Anderson, got pally with him, and took advantage of this burgeoning of a beautiful friendship to shove me off on him in the capacity, as I say, of a desk clerk. Came the dawn, and J. G. Anderson gave me what Potter calls the old heave-ho."

"Wouldn't he take you back?"

Barmy laughed a faint, weak laugh. He had not supposed that he would ever again be capable of laughter, even of the faint, weak type, but this artless question succeeded in producing it.

"If I read aright the message in his eyes when we parted, no. But, dash it, we mustn't waste time talking about jobs and the distant future. We've got to decide what to tell J. Bromley Lippincott. He'll be back in about two shakes, all agog to know what the score is. We shall have to tell him something."

Dinty reflected.

"Suppose you gave him what he wanted?"

"It wouldn't leave much to split up."

"That's true."

"Half of thirty-three and one-third per centum per me per Oscar per person." Barmy paced the floor feverishly. Remorse was searing him. "It makes me feel such an abysmal louse, having got Oscar into the thing. There he was, poor broken blossom, perfectly happy, with a good job and all that money in the old sock, and I come barging in and . . . Holy smoke!" said Barmy, as knuckles rapped on the door. "That can't be J. Bromley already, can it?"

"Come in," said Dinty. "No, of course it can't. He won't be here for another twenty minutes. It's probably . . . Oh, hello, Mr. Potter."

"Oh, hullo," said Barmy.

Although the party given in his honour on the previous night by a few friends and admirers had not broken up till six in the morning, Mervyn Potter was looking extraordinarily spruce and debonair. His eye was not dimmed nor his natural force abated. He was one of those fortunate persons who seem to thrive on a shortage of sleep. If there was any criticism that could have been made of his appearance, it was that though the day was well advanced, it being now nearly lunch-time, he was still wearing the white tie and tails more conventionally allotted to the dinner hour. And the bizarre note was further stressed by the circumstance that some loving hand had written the words 'Oh, baby!' across his shirt front in lipstick.

But Mervyn Potter was never the man to attach too much importance to the trivialities of dress. If you had asked him, he would have said that it was the soul that mattered. 'Get the soul functioning in mid-season form,' he would have told you, 'and the outer crust can take care of itself.' He beamed upon his old friend Barmy, and his young friend Dinty, and asked if they had read the notices.

"A genuine triumph," said Mervyn Potter, "reflecting great credit on all concerned. We shall run a year. But I didn't come simply to tell you that, gratifying though it admittedly is. I am here, Phipps, old friend, in the capacity of an ambassador. I'll sit down, if you don't mind. Is anybody except the great white chief allowed to use that swivel chair? Throw me out if I'm breaking the rules."

He seated himself at the desk, and put his feet on it.

"Yes," he resumed, "I am a plenipotentiary. One of those boys who go in for pourparlers. I have been asked to treat with you in a matter of considerable importance. I was curled up on the floor of my bedroom at the Lambs this morning, sleeping like a little child," explained Mervyn Potter, "when the telephone rang from downstairs and I was informed that I had a visitor. 'Strangle him with your bare hands,' I said. They doubted whether this could be done. 'Then send the hellhound up,' I said, and they sent up the hellhound. And who do you think it was, this hound of hell? None other than our old crony, J. G. Anderson, of the Skeewassett Andersons. And after the customary civilities had been exchanged, he asked me to plead with you to buy that hotel of his. I gather that a previous meeting you found yourself unable to ante up, but now that you have made this colossal hit, pulling in millions weekly, he feels that the conversations can be resumed. He'll take seventy-five thousand, he says."

"Ha!"

"I beg your pardon? What did you say?"

"Just Ha!" said Barmy.

Mervyn Potter was puzzled.

"You say Ha! thereby placing yourself in a limited class with
the war-horse which, if you recall, made the same observation
among the trumpets, but what does it *mean*? Enlarge on that
simple ejaculation."

Barmy went to the water-cooler and filled a paper cup.

"When he said seventy-five thousand, did he mean dollars
or cents?"

"Dollars, I understood."

"Well, it doesn't much matter," said Barmy, "because even
seventy-five thousand cents would be beyond the scope of the
privy purse."

"We've had bad news, Mr. Potter," said Dinty. "Tell him,
Barmy."

Brokenly, Barmy told the story, and Mervyn Potter, shaking
his head, agreed that 'bad' was a neat description.

"What are you going to do?" he asked.

"We don't know. We were just talking it over when you
arrived."

"I fear you will have to give him his pound of flesh. Lawyers,"
said Mervyn Potter, "are the devil. Back in Hollywood I moved
in a morass of them. They were about my board and about my
bed, spying out all my ways. I remember once——"

What it was that Mervyn Potter remembered was not destined
to be revealed, for at this moment the door flew open and Fanny
Lehman swept in with that confident stride of hers which always
gave the impression that she was taking the stage preparatory
to wowing an audience with six clubs at the finish. She seemed
in the highest spirits. Her eyes were bright, her face aglow. She
looked like a woman about to slip something over on somebody.

"Hello, children," she said. "Hello, Mr. Potter."

"Good morning, madam."

The last thing Barmy wanted at this moment, with problems
to be threshed out and vital decisions arrived at, was an interruption, even from a woman of whom he had always been fond.
But if short on the little grey cells, he was courteous.

"Oh, hullo, Mrs. Lehman," he said, and hoped that the words

had not sounded like a death-rattle.

They had. Fanny's eyebrows rose. Her eyes shot from him to to Dinty and back again. She was a quick observer, and even a slow observer would have sensed a strain in the atmosphere.

"For heaven's sake!" she said. "What's all this about? You ought to be peppier than this. Don't you know you've got a hit?"

"Oh, rather. Yes, I know that all right."

"Well, I'm here to tell you that you've got about three times as big a hit as you think you have. It's that brothel scene that's rung the bell. The police are going to try to close the show on account of it, and you know what that means. You'll have 'em hanging on to the rafters."

Barmy gasped. What with J. Bromley Lippincott and the New York police force, he was feeling like an electric hare pursued by an army corps of greyhounds.

"But suppose they do close it?"

Fanny laughed indulgently.

"Not a chance. Not in this town."

"No," said Mervyn Potter. "New York isn't Boston. We got our rights here, boy. All that will happen is that there will be a lot of front-page stuff in the papers and you'll have to cut out a couple of 'Hells' and a 'Damn' or two tomorrow night. You will then put them back on the following night and carry on as before."

"And meanwhile," said Fanny, "every single individual person in the city with four dollars eighty in his kick will come burning up the sidewalks to get at the box office window."

"While those who haven't four dollars eighty," said Mervyn Potter, "will run around in circles till they've borrowed it somewhere."

"I tell you," said Fanny, "it's going to be a landslide. And I'll tell you something else. You've got company coming."

"Eh?" said Barmy. "Company?"

"Mr. Lehman."

Dinty uttered a cry.

"Mr. Lehman?"

"None other. He's smoked out a bankroll," said Fanny, giving full weight to the announcement, "and he wants to buy the show back. He raised the money on that tip about the police, and he's got it with him in certified cheques."

If she had expected the news to make a sensation, she was not disappointed. Barmy gasped, and looked at Dinty. Dinty gasped, and looked at Barmy. To both of them simultaneously a thought had come like a full-blown rose, flushing the brow.   And it was plain from his demeanour that the same thought had come to Mervyn Potter.

"Golly!" said Dinty.

"The happy ending," said Mervyn Potter.

"It will be if he doesn't get here in less than about a quarter of a hour," said Barmy. "Will he get here in less than about a quarter of an hour?" he asked tensely.

Fanny looked puzzled.

"What's all this?" she asked. "What's going on?"

Barmy pressed his point.

"Will he, do you think?"

"I guess so. He's on his way. I just shot ahead of him to give you the low-down. I got a kind of fool liking for you, brother Phipps. Somehow, suckers always appealed to me. And I don't think Joe Lehman ought to be encouraged to slip the harpoon into the young and innocent. Joe's swell, and I love him, but I don't like some of his ways."

"How true," said Mervyn Potter. "They do invite criticism. I don't know where Joe got his early education, but it was in some school or college where they forgot to teach him the difference between right and wrong. There is a difference, so they tell me, but nobody ever straightened Joe out on it."

"No," said Fanny. "He's planning the steal of the century, bless his impetuous old heart, and I raced ahead to warn you. When he arrives and goes into his act, don't weaken for a single instant. If you let that robber baron sweet-talk you into parting with this show, it'll be a crime."

Somebody banged on the door. Fanny smiled a gentle smile.

"Ah! Up goes the curtain!"

"Yes," said Mervyn Potter. "Here, if I mistake not, Watson, is our client now."

★ 21 ★

WHEN Mr. Lehman came lumbering in, a man in a hurry, the first emotion he experienced was one of surprise at finding himself a unit of what appeared to be some sort of convention. The magnitude of the crowd in his old office plainly took him aback. He looked at Barmy. He looked at Dinty. He looked at Mervyn Potter. Then his gaze fell upon Fanny, and he started like one who finds tarantulas in his bath tub.

"You!" he said, speaking hoarsely. "What are you doing here?"

"Just visiting."

"Get out!"

Barmy raised his eyebrows. One cannot have this sort of thing.

"Hoy!" he said, with quiet rebuke. "You're not going to start putting people out of places again, are you? This is *my* office," said Barmy. "Fourteen Hundred and Sixty-Eight Broadway, New York, New York, A New York corporation, and any putting out of people that's required, I'll attend to—by my halidom."

"Well spoken, Phipps," said Mervyn Potter.

"The word in season, what?"

"Right plumb spang in season," said Mervyn Potter.

Barmy seated himself in the swivel chair which Mervyn Potter had gallantly vacated on Fanny's entrance, and put his feet on the desk.

"Sit down, sweetheart," he said, "and let's hear what's on your mind."

"Such as it is," said Mervyn Potter.

"Precisely," said Barmy. "Such as it is. What brings you here this bright, sunny morning, my blossom?"

Mr. Lehman, who during these exchanges had been glowering at the wife of his bosom, turned to him with a passionate gesture.

"Listen," he said. "I don't know what she's been handing you, but don't start believing it."

"You speak in riddles, laddie."

"Look," said Mr. Lehman. "I come around to give you your coin back—let you out clean."

"You mean you want to buy the show?"

"I'll give you what you paid for it—twenty thousand. You won't lose a thing."

"You won't either, will you, what?"

"What?"

"That's what I said. What?"

"I don't get you."

Barmy had never expected that the time would come when he would be glad to have met J. Bromley Lippincott, but he was conscious now of a marked thankfulness that he had been privileged to see the attorney-at-law in action, for there was much which a young theatrical manager could learn from that dark, cadaverous man in the matter of deportment. He could not make himself dark and cadaverous, but he could borrow some of the steel and thrust of J. Bromley Lippincott's manner, and he did so.

"Let me explain," he said. "You talk airily——"

"Or glibly," said Mervyn Potter.

"Or, of course, glibly," assented Barmy, always open to suggestions. "You talk airily or glibly of buying the show, but let me remind you that the aforesaid dramatic composition—or play—is a dashed valuable property. It's the greatest dramatic novelty in twenty years. It starts with a Prologue——"

Mr. Lehman exploded.

"You're going to believe that stuff of hers, huh? Listen, my blossom——"

"I'm listening, my puss."

"I'm an old hand at this game. Huh?"

The 'Huh?' was addressed to Fanny, who had uttered the words 'Vaudeville agent'. On request, she repeated them, and Mr. Lehman, scorching her with a malignant stare, said "That's all right about Vaudeville agents, we aren't talking about Vaudeville agents, we're talking about running shows."

"I'm an old hand at this game," he said again, striking the palm of his left hand with the clenched fist of his right, "and I can make something out of this show, but you can't."

"I can't?"

"No."

Barmy uttered a light laugh. J. Bromley Lippincott in a similar situation would, he was aware, have frowned, but he preferred the light laugh. It did not tinkle quite so musically as he could have wished, so he tried it over again, and this time it tinkled splendidly.

"I can't, eh? Step round to the theatre and take a look·at the mob of pleasure-seekers trying to buy tickets. It's a whale of a hit, sweetheart, and under my management——"

"It's the management that counts," said Mervyn Potter.

"Yessir, it's the management that counts," said Barmy. "Absolutely. You need the expert hand, and that's what this dramatic production's got nothing else but of."

Mr. Lehman was breathing in a stertorous manner which would have caused his doctor to purse his lips and reach for the sedatives.

"Look," he said. "I'll give you thirty, and I've got the certified cheques in my pocket. Set?"

Barmy shook his head.

"It can't be done, old son. For your own sake I couldn't do it. If you had it on your conscience that you had sweet-talked me into selling a big dramatic novelty like this for thirty thousand dollars, you'd never have a moment's peace. You wouldn't sleep at nights. There's a cabaret scene——"

"Forty."

"Sorry."

"I only got fifty. Do you want it all? Do you think I'm trying to gyp you?"

"No, no. I acquit you of any deliberate malice aforethought. Unfortunately——"

At this point, there was a sound like a mighty rushing wind, the door flew open, and Jack McClure came whirling in, not stopping to knock. Like his late partner, he appeared to be in a hurry. Seeing Mr. Lehman, he rocked back on his heels, shocked and astounded.

"So!" he said, with a wealth of emotion in his voice.

"Aha!" said Fanny. "The boy friend!"

"I thought so!" said Jack McClure, and not even J. Bromley Lippincott, appalled by a whale of a case of plagiarism, could have put more horror and indignation into three short words. "Trying to doublecross me, eh?" said Jack McClure. His burning eyes rested on Mr. Lehman for a long moment, then he wrenched them away and turned to Barmy. "Have you sold it to him yet?"

"The big dramatic novelty?"

Jack McClure, generally so quiet and gentlemanly, raised his voice to a shout.

"If you haven't, don't. Because he's out to skin you."

"Mr. Lehman?" said Barmy, amazed.

"He didn't tell you about the police, did he?"

"I did," said Fanny, and Mr. Lehman gave her a look which J. Bromley Lippincott, had he been present to observe it, would have been the first to admit surpassed by a long way anything in his own *repertoire*.

"Just a pal!" he said thickly. "Just a pal!"

Jack McClure was getting down to business.

"Look here. I'll give you fifty thousand dollars. I've got it right here."

"Fifty thousand?" Barmy risked the tinkling laugh again. "Why, even Mr. Lehman offered that."

"He did?"

"Do you want to go any higher? It's a terrific dramatic composition. A priest comes in with a rabbi, and they gab back and forth—and so on and so on——"

Jack McClure fingered his chin.

"Fifty thousand? That's a lot of dough."

"How about you, Mr. Lehman?"

Mr. Lehman's attention had been momentarily detached from the discussion. He was telling his wife in a low, confidential undertone that he intended to brain her. It was Mervyn Potter who took it upon himself to offer a suggestion.

"I think——" said Mervyn Potter, and paused. For the first time this morning he had caught a glimpse of his shirt front and read its message. He stiffened, and there came into his handsome face a keen, accusing look. "Lehman," he said, "is this your handiwork? Was it you who crept up on me like a thief in the night and wrote the words 'Oh, baby!' on my wishbone?" Then, softening, he went on: "No, of course you didn't. You don't use lipstick, do you? I imagine the thing will have to remain one of those insoluble historic mysteries like the man in the iron mask. But I was saying I think I see the way out. I don't know if you have had much to do with the world of finance, but I believe that on these occasions when two tycoons, call them Tycoon A. and Tycoon B., are desirous of putting through some important deal and neither will yield to the other, they frequently settle the difficulty by resorting to what is known as a merger. They, as it were, if you follow me, merge. It seems to me that this would be an admirable way of adjusting the present problem. You, my plutocratic old Lehman, have fifty thousand dollars. You, my wealthy old McClure, possess the same. Why don't you pool your pieces of eight and buy the show together?"

Barmy was lost in admiration. King Solomon, he told himself, was a fool to this clear thinker. Right from the moment when Jack McClure had mentioned that fifty thousand, he had had a feeling, watching Mervyn Potter out of the corner of his eye, that the motion picture star was about to come forward with an idea of some kind, a notion of sorts, a ruse of some description. And now he had done so, and every word that had fallen from his lips had been an Orient pearl of purest rays serene.

"That's the stuff!" he cried buoyantly. "Hats off to M. Potter, the man with the bulging forehead. One hundred thousand is the price, Mr. Lehman. How about it?"

Mr. Lehman sank into a chair. Jack McClure did the same.

"A hundred thousand?" said Mr. Lehman.

"A hundred thousand?" said Jack McClure.

"And think on your feet," said Barmy.

Mr. Lehman rose like a rocket. So did Jack McClure.

"Is that . . ." Mr. Lehman gulped. In the past minute or two he appeared to have aged a good deal. He might have been the elder brother of the man who had burst into the room so short a while before, an elder brother who had led a hard life and seen a lot of trouble and was wearing a collar some sizes too small for him. "Is that final?"

"Absolutely final."

"Five-star," said Fanny, and received from her mate another look which would have extorted generous admiration from that specialist in dirty looks, J. Bromley Lippincott.

"Of course, I must know right away," said Barmy. He snapped his fingers. "That's the show game!"

Mr. Lehman tottered to the door of Dinty's cubby-hole.

"Come in here a minute, Jack."

"Okay."

"We'll be right back," said Mr. Lehman.

The cubbyhole door closed behind them. Fanny drew a deep breath.

"And I came here to look after you!" she said.

Dinty went to her, her face glowing.

"We couldn't have done a thing without you, Mrs. Lehman," she said. "We do appreciate it . . . enormously. Don't we, Barmy?"

"I'll never forget it, dear old present help in time of trouble," said Barmy fervently. "You will receive favourable mention in my prayers night and morning from now onward, and the first Phipps issue shall be named after you. If a girl of course. If male, Mervyn, after Potter."

"You could find no nobler label for a bouncing baby," said Mervyn Potter.

"Issue?" said Fanny.

"Just peeping into Vol Two," Barmy explained. "Dinty and I are going to be married."

"Is that so?"

"Well, well," said Mervyn Potter. "So you're getting married, eh? Starting out on the new life together, you two young things, are you? I wish you every luck and happiness. But it is a very moot point," he proceeded, striking a graver note, "whether a girl who marries a man with two names isn't committing bigamy. I see certain embarrassments ahead of you, young Dinty Moore. You may feel a bit silly one of these long winter evenings when you are sitting on Fotheringay's lap and Phipps suddenly comes in, or vice versa. Still, that is entirely your own affair, entirely your own affair. I just thought I would mention it."

Fanny was eyeing Barmy with open admiration.

"And to think that I ever took you for a sucker! You've certainly put it over. You must have had second sight when you insisted on buying that play. But how it ever turned out to be a hit will always be a mystery to your Aunt Sadie. If you see what I mean, Mr. Potter."

"I see precisely what you mean," said Mervyn Potter. "But we must never forget that not only was it presented by Cyril Phipps, with all the advantages of the inimitable Phipps touch, but it had as its star one whom, did not modesty forbid, I would describe as——"

"A ham?"

"You take the words out of my mouth, dear lady. And talking of mouths, mine is so singularly dry that if I do not immediately lubricate it, I shall have another of those dust bowls on my hands. You would not care to accompany me around the corner and hoist a few?"

"It's a lie," said Fanny. "I would and will."

"I always say that there is nothing like a little something at about this hour of the morning to pick one up," said Mervyn Potter. "Good-bye, young Dinty. Good-bye—for the present— my old friend Phipps. I shall inform J. G. Anderson that he will shortly be seeing you. He is awaiting me at a certain bar not far from here. Give me half an hour, and I think I can get him so oiled that he will slice the price of that hotel of his practically to nothing. When you are through in here, if you wish to talk business with our Anderson, turn to the left as you leave the building, walk down a couple of blocks till you come to a bistro called Mike's Place, and wait outside till you hear rowdy drinking songs proceeding from its interior. That will be J. G. Anderson, and that will be the moment to strike."

And with an old-world courtesy Mervyn Potter escorted Fanny from the room. As the door closed, they could hear him explaining to her that the words 'Oh, baby!' on his shirt front were in his opinion probably the work of an international gang and that he thought he knew the ringleaders.

"What a man!" said Dinty.

Barmy did not reply. A reaction had come upon him. Dominant a moment ago, he was suffering now from those unmanning tremors which so often poisoned the day for Oscar Fritchie. Once, visiting Monte Carlo, he had placed his last hundred francs on the red at the roulette table, and it was with the emotions with which he had watched the wheel begin to spin that he now gazed at the door behind which the two tycoons were holding their conference. For comfort and moral support he turned, as he was always to turn for the rest of a long life, to Dinty.

"Do you think they'll do it?"

"Of course they will."

"But suppose that lawyer comes back before they decide?"

He broke off. Oscar Fritchie was sliding in in that odd, crab-like way of his which always suggested that he was expecting something—the ceiling, as it might be, or possibly a thunderbolt—to fall on his head. Oscar had had three quick ones at Mike's Place, but though filled with the old familiar juice he was still the timid, palpitating rabbit which might have come—though actually as we have seen, it did not—out of J. Bromley Lippincott's briefcase. Looking about him and seeing no sign of Mr. Lippincott, he perked up for an instant. Then, as a booming voice came through the door of the cubbyhole, he sagged again.

"He's in there, is he?" he said despondently.

"No, Mr. Lippincott's gone," said Dinty. "He's coming back again——"

"Oh?" said Oscar, even more despondently.

"—but he's not here now. That's Mr. Lehman and Mr. McClure in there.

"Lehman and McClure? What are they doing here? Gosh!" said Oscar Fritchie, seeing it all. "There was something wrong with those papers we signed and they didn't sell us the show."

"Yes, they did," said Barmy. "And now they want to buy it back. I'm asking a hundred thousand."

"What!"

"Yah."

"A hundred thousand *dollars?*"

"Yah."

"Jiminy Christmas!" said Oscar Fritchie.

Barmy's momentary weakness had passed. Once more he was the man who thought on his feet and made quick decisions.

"Listen, my quivering aspen," he said. "What you might call the whole aspect of the fruity old situation has changed. Lehman and McClure have come here with certified cheques clutched in their hot little hands, and it is but a matter of time before we shall have a hundred thousand of the best and brightest at our disposal. And my late employer, J. G. Anderson, is waiting for me down the street to sell me his hotel in Bessemer, Ohio. You and I'll buy it together, what? We can make it one of the greatest dramatic hotels in the world, anywhere. You don't want to be in show business. Does he?"

"Of course not," said Dinty.

"Don't I?" said Oscar.

"Certainly not," said Barmy. "A man like you should be in the hotel business. Shouldn't he?"

"Of course he should."

"But last time you said I ought to get out of it."

"Oh, that was different," said Barmy. "You'll like Bessemer. It's a wonderful place. Look! I'll sell you twenty-five per cent of the hotel for your share of the hundred thousand. Set?"

"Well . . . now . . ."

Barmy rapped the desk.

"Come on, come on. Think on your feet. It's a deal?"

It would have taken a better man than Oscar Fritchie to resist
this high-powered salesmanship, particularly at a moment when
Dinty was clutching the lapel of his coat and looking yearningly
into his eyes.

"Well, if you say so," he said weakly.

"Right!" said Barmy, and Mr. Lehman and Jack McClure
came out of the cubbyhole. They had the air of men who have
arrived, not perhaps without reluctance, at a decision.

"Oh, hello," said Oscar. "Hello, Mr. Lehman. Hello, Mr.
McClure."

"How are you?" said Jack McClure.

"Not bad. I've a funny kind of buzzing feeling in my head and
my throat's sort of——"

"Please!" said Barmy, rightly considering that these details
should more properly be reserved for Oscar Fritchie's medical
adviser. "Well?" he said, turning to Mr. Lehman.

Mr. Lehman seemed to have a lingering hope that something
might be accomplished by a last appeal to Barmy's better feelings.

"Now, look here a minute——"

He stopped. An authoritative knock had sounded on the door.
Barmy and Dinty exchanged an agonized glance. They did not
need to be told who was on the other side of that door. The half-
hour was up, and J. Bromley Lippincott, of Lippincott, Lippincott, Cohn, Mandelbaum and Lippincott, attorneys-at-law, was
with them once again. He might have dallied over a drink at the
Astor bar, he might have sauntered up Broadway, seeing the
sights, he might have done a hundred things which would have
made him late at the tryst, but no. He had returned at the
appointed time, punctual to the second.

"I'll go," said Oscar, ever obliging, heading for the door.

"No, no!" cried Barmy in agony, seizing his coat.

"Huh?"

Barmy swallowed.

"It's . . . it's only . . . I know who it is." He reached the door
in a single bound and turned the key. A moment for mopping
the brow, and he was back with Mr. Lehman again. "What were
you going to say?" he asked, his fingers busy with his tie.

Oscar Fritchie was not the man to give up easily. He had seen
a chance of being helpful, and he hated to let it go.

"But if there's somebody out there——"

"There isn't anybody out there."

The knock was repeated, louder and more authoritative than ever.

"Well, I'll take your word for it," said Oscar Fritchie doubtfully, a puzzled eye on the door.

"Who's out there?" said Mr. Lehman.

"It isn't anybody," said Barmy, whose tie was now a mere tangle. "It's just a book agent or something, I expect. Well, do you want the show or don't you?" he demanded desperately.

"Well, now, look here, sweetheart. A hundred grand, that's a big bundle of coin. You can't expect us to . . ." Mr. Lehman broke off as the echoes of a third knock boomed through the room. "For heaven's sake," he barked irritably, "why don't you send that pest away?"

Dinty took over the conduct of affairs with the quiet, efficient smoothness so characteristic of women when they are about to embark on a course of action not scrupulously honest. It was plain to her that her Barmy was unequal to coping with the situation, and it was a situation which, with a little feminine manipulation of the truth, could so easily be handled.

"Mr. Phipps can't send him away," she said. "Would you like to know who he is?"

"I don't care who he is, as long as he stops his racket."

"It's a man who wants to take over most of the show," said Dinty carelessly.

Mr. Lehman tottered.

"What!"

"You'd be surprised if you knew his name. He's a man who does things just like that," said Dinty, snapping her fingers. "So if you don't want the show, just say the word and I'll let him in."

"Wait!" cried Mr. Lehman. "Wait! Wait! Wait! Wait! Wait!"

With a feverish haste he pulled out his certified cheque, but no more rapidly than Jack McClure produced his. With a simultaneous movement, as if they had been rehearsing for weeks, they thrust them upon Barmy, and Barmy dutifully handed them to Dinty, who had been busily scribbling on a piece of paper.

"Now it's ours!" said Mr. Lehman.

"And here's your receipt," said Dinty.

"And I get my money back?" said Oscar anxiously.

"My dear old prune," said Barmy, who had made another of his quick recoveries and was now at the peak of his form again, "you get a lot more. I explained it carefully to you a moment ago, but I suppose it didn't penetrate. The Lehman-McClure comedy duo have paid a hundred thousand dollars——"

"For thirty-three and one-third per centum of the show," said Dinty.

Mr. Lehman started violently.

"For *what*?"

"This gentleman will tell you all about it," said Dinty, throwing open the door, and J. Bromley Lippincott entered, looking, if possible, taller and darker and more cadaverous than ever.

"He's a lawyer," said Barmy. "At law. And he wants sixty-six and two-thirds per centum of all profits derived from aforesaid play, when, if and as produced, because aforesaid play was pinched bodily from a novelette written by his client, Mr. Rodney Rich of Worcester, Massachusetts, a Massachusetts corporation. It's a clear case of plagiarism, and one of the most flagrant that it has ever been Pop Lippincott's privilege to encounter. Correct, my old crumpet?"

"Perfectly correct," said his old crumpet. "Who are these gentlemen?"

"Mr. Lehman and Mr. McClure. They've just bought the show back again."

"Indeed?"

"Yes, indeed," said Oscar Fritchie emphatically. He wished for no misunderstanding on this point. On others, possibly, but not on this one.

Mr. Lehman, gallant in defeat, was making a Custer's Last Stand.

"I know all about this phony case," he said. "You ain't got no more grounds than a rabbit."

J. Bromley Lippincott did not smile. Attorneys-at-law do not smile. But a quick muscular spasm at the corner of his tight-drawn lips seemed to indicate that he had come as near to smiling as an attorney-at-law ever comes.

"We have a perfect case," he said composedly.

"Yah? Well, come in here and tell us all about it," said Mr. Lehman, "and see how quick I'll turn that perfect case of yours inside out. There ain't been a hit produced in twenty years that some guy ain't said it was swiped from him."

He led the way into the cubbyhole, his whole air that of a good man wronged. Jack McClure, about to follow, lingered for an instant, giving Barmy a reproachful look.

"You have disappointed me," said Jack McClure.

He went into the cubbyhole, and the door closed behind him. As it shut, J. Bromley Lippincott could be heard saying . . . at one hundred and forty-six points.

Barmy had become brisk and executive.

"Hey!" he said.

"Me?" said Oscar Fritchie.

"Yah. Do you know the Guaranty Trust Company, Forty-Third Street and Fifth Avenue?"

"No."

"Well, it's there. Fifth Avenue and Forty-Third Street. Rush along there and deposit these cheques without the loss of a single instant. Fly like a youthful hart or roe over the hills where spices grow. Lehman might take it into his head to stop them. By bunging them in like a flash of lightning, we avoid all rannygazoo."

"And one does so wish, does one not," said Dinty, "to avoid rannygazoo. Why don't you deposit them yourself, *maitre?*"

"I have one or two letters, cables and telegrams to get off," said Barmy. "Got that clear? Tell me in your own words what you're supposed to do."

"Go to the bank——"

"—and deposit the cheques to account of Cyril Phipps. Right. And now do you know a joint called Mike's Place?"

"I just come from there."

"Good. After you've been to the bank, go to Mike's Place. You will see there, in company with Mervyn Potter, an elderly man with a face like a passport photograph. His name is J. G. Anderson. Tell him I'll be along in a minute. He's the bloke who owns the hotel we're going to buy. Set?"

"Okay," said Oscar. He would have preferred to remain and ask a lot of questions, but even he could see that this matter of depositing the cheques was one of urgency. He left the room at what for him was a rapid pace.

"And I'll tell you something more about this show," Mr. Lehman was shouting in the cubbyhole. "There was a fellow called George Bernard Shaw——"

Barmy turned to Dinty, as brisk as ever.

"Can you do shorthand?"

"The shorter it is, the better I like it."

"Take a cable," said Barmy curtly. "To Theodore, Lord Binghampton, Binghampton Hall, Binghampton, Norfolk,

England. 'Letter received and torn into a thousand pieces. Go and boil your bally head, sweetheart. Cheerio. Cyril'."

"Is that all?"

"That's all. Now a telegram. To the Rector, or Vicar or whatever he is, Little Church Around The Corner . . . where?"

"Twenty-Ninth Street."

"Twenty-Ninth Street. 'What ho, vicar, or rector as the case may be. Clear decks for big wedding in near future, my puss. The Phippses are coming—and I may add with bells on. Regards. Phipps'."

"You do write such lovely telegrams."

"And now a letter. To the President, White Star Cunard Line. Where do we find the President, White Star Cunard Line?"

"Somewhere down at the bottom of Broadway."

"Right. To the President White Star Cunard Line, somewhere at the bottom of Broadway. 'Dear Sir. Kindly quote me your lowest terms for the liner Queen Mary . . .'."

Barmy paused. He blinked like an awakened somnambulist.

"I'm crazy," he said. "We aren't buying ocean liners, we're buying hotels. Omit letter to President White Star Cunard Line, somewhere down at the bottom of Broadway, slip me one quick kiss for the road, then ho, for the great open spaces!"

In the cubbyhole, Mr. Lehman was making a telling point.

"And another thing. The man in that novelette was named George. In the play he's Harold . . ."

But Dinty and Barmy missed this. They were already on their way to Mike's Place.